"I LIKE TO SEE THINGS GROW . . ."

She smiled as she said it, her mist-gray eyes simmering as she leaned forward to meet Fargo. He pressed his mouth to hers, worked her lips open, and tasted the warm wetness of her tongue. Her arms slid around his neck and she held tight as he let his tongue probe, slowly first, in a tantalizing circle. He felt her own tongue respond, slipping forward to meet his, explore, taste, ask. His hand pressed down over one creamy mound, pushing the neckline of the dress down; he felt her reach up, fingers finding a snap and the front of the dress coming open. He drew back to gaze at the full beauty of her for a moment. Then, feeling his desire growing indeed, he reached for her again . . .

SIGNET Westerns You'll Enjoy

☐ **THE TRAILSMAN #1: SEVEN WAGONS WEST by Jon Sharpe.**
(#E9307—$1.75)*
☐ **THE TRAILSMAN #2: THE HANGING TRAIL by Jon Sharpe.**
(#E9308—$1.75)*
☐ **THE TRAILSMAN #3: MOUNTAIN MAN KILL by Jon Sharpe.**
(#E9353—$1.75)*
☐ **THE TRAILSMAN #4: THE SUNDOWN SEARCHERS by Jon Sharpe.**
(#E9533—$1.75)*
☐ **THE TRAILSMAN #5: THE RIVER RAIDERS by Jon Sharpe.**
(#AE1199—$2.25)*
☐ **THE ANGRY HORSEMEN by Lewis B. Patten.** (#E9309—$1.75)
☐ **PURSUIT by Lewis B. Patten.** (#E9209—$1.75)
☐ **SIGNET DOUBLE WESTERN—LAWMAN FOR SLAUGHTER VALLEY by Ray Hogan and PASSAGE TO DODGE CITY by Ray Hogan.** (#J9173—$1.95)*
☐ **SIGNET DOUBLE WESTERN—BRANDON'S POSSE by Ray Hogan and THE HELL MERCHANT by Ray Hogan.**
(#J8857—$1.95)*
☐ **THE RAPTORS by Ray Hogan.** (#E9124—$1.75)
☐ **THE DEAD GUN by Ray Hogan.** (#E9026—$1.75)
☐ **SIGNET DOUBLE WESTERN—PATCHSADDLE DRIVE by Cliff Farrell and SHOOTOUT AT SIOUX WELLS by Cliff Farrell.**
(#J9258—$1.95)*
☐ **SIGNET DOUBLE WESTERN—APACHE HOSTAGE by Lewis B. Patten and LAW OF THE GUN by Lewis B. Patten.**
(#J9420—$1.95)
☐ **SIGNET DOUBLE WESTERN—SADDLE AND RIDE by Ernest Haycox and THE FEUDISTS by Ernest Haycox.**
(#J9467—$1.95)
☐ **SIGNET DOUBLE WESTERN—RIM OF THE DESERT by Ernest Haycox and DEAD MAN RANGE by Ernest Haycox.**
(#J9210—$1.95)

*Price slightly higher in Canada

THE TRAILSMAN 8

SIX-GUN DRIVE

by

Jon Sharpe

A SIGNET BOOK

NEW AMERICAN LIBRARY

TIMES MIRROR

NAL BOOKS ARE AVAILABLE AT QUANTITY DISCOUNTS WHEN USED TO PROMOTE PRODUCTS OR SERVICES. FOR INFORMATION PLEASE WRITE TO PREMIUM MARKETING DIVISION, THE NEW AMERICAN LIBRARY, INC., 1633 BROADWAY, NEW YORK, NEW YORK 10019.

Copyright © 1981 by Jon Sharpe

The first chapter of this book appeared in *Wolf Country*, the seventh volume of this series.

SIGNET TRADEMARK REG. U.S. PAT. OFF. AND FOREIGN COUNTRIES REGISTERED TRADEMARK—MARCA REGISTRADA HECHO EN CHICAGO, U.S.A.

SIGNET, SIGNET CLASSICS, MENTOR, PLUME, MERIDIAN AND NAL BOOKS are published by The New American Library, Inc., 1633 Broadway, New York, New York 10019

First Printing, October, 1981

1 2 3 4 5 6 7 8 9

PRINTED IN THE UNITED STATES OF AMERICA

The Trailsman

Beginnings . . . they bend the tree and they mark the man. Skye Fargo was born when he was eighteen. Terror was his midwife, vengeance his first cry. Killing spawned Skye Fargo, ruthless, cold-blooded murder. Out of the acrid smoke of gunpowder still hanging in the air, he rose, cried out a promise never forgotten.

The Trailsman, they began to call him all across the West, searcher, scout, hunter, the man who could see where others only looked, his skills for hire but not his soul, the man who lived each day to the fullest, yet trailed each tomorrow. Skye Fargo, the Trailsman, the seeker who could take the wildness of a land and the wanting of a woman and make them his own.

*The Kansas territory,
north of the
Smoky Hill River—1861*

Pretty did not fit her. Beautiful was too strong. Handsome, Fargo decided, she was a handsome girl, even from a distance. He'd watched her for almost a week, now, from his vantage point atop the hill and under the thick leaves of the ironwood. Every morning she rode to the shallow land at the bottom of the hill to work the horse. It was the ritual that first made him curious, then fascinated. And made him look at her more carefully.

A tall girl, she had a lithe, narrow-hipped body with smallish breasts and a way of walking with her hips slightly thrust forward. He couldn't make out the color of her eyes but she had an angular face, strong yet no rawbonedness in it, with good planes, an intense kind of handsomeness. Light-brown hair hung long and tied behind her to flash coppery glintings in the morning sun.

This morning was the same as the others, the big black-haired man saw as she appeared at one end of the shallow land, swung down from the horse, and took a jar of oil from her saddlebag. She rubbed the horse's legs with it. That was the beginning of the ritual. She followed with a towel, drying the oil that remained glistening on the horse's legs, then used a stable rubber over the animal. Next she remounted, rode the horse to a point, and then sent her mount into a galloping start, racing in a long circle, taking three hurdles, a fallen log, a hedge, and a high-standing tree stump. She jumped well and made two runs of what was obviously a mock race course. Halting, she took out a pocket watch and consulted the piece, then dismounted and walked the horse down in a tight circle.

The horse was a dark bay, mostly quarterhorse, Fargo guessed, thick-chested and strong enough. He had good speed, enough to take most horses of his kind, Fargo mused, and his glance flicked to his own horse, the pinto standing well back under the trees, a striking Ovaro, shining jet-black forequarters and hindquarters and gleaming white midsection. The Ovaro could easily outrun the girl's horse, he felt certain, returned his eyes to the girl as she finished cooling her steed.

She was about to remount the horse when the three riders appeared. They came charging out of a thicket of red ash and Fargo saw the girl spin around to face them. One, clad in a dirty brown shirt, swung a lariat around the horse's neck, pulled the animal to the side. A second man with a flat-brimmed black hat tossed a second lariat on the horse. The third one leaped to the ground and Fargo saw the flat length of plank in his hand. As the girl screamed, he began to smash the plank against the horse's legs as the other two kept the horse from bolting.

Fargo was on the pinto, starting to race downhill as he saw the girl leap onto the one with the board, sink her teeth into his arm, and rake her nails across his face. "Bastard. Stinking, rotten bastard," he heard her scream.

"Ow, Jesus," the man yelped, whirled, flung her off, and kicked her as she tried to get up. He aimed another kick at her and the girl wrapped her arms around his leg, pulled him off balance, and he fell to one knee. She was up at once, racing to the lariats, tugging at them.

"Let that horse go, you bastards," she screamed. Fargo reached the spot as the third man grabbed her arms, yanked them back of her, and she gasped in

2

pain. The man started to turn as he heard the pinto galloping toward him, was too late to avoid Fargo's arm as it shot out, smashed him across the side of the head. The man toppled to the ground and Fargo leaped from the pinto as the dirty brown shirt pulled his lariat from the horse, started to wheel around. He avoided a swiping blow, grabbed the man's arm and yanked and the rider flew out of the saddle to land on his hands and knees.

He started to turn, reach for the gun at his side. Fargo's kick caught his gun hand and the man gasped in pain as he toppled sideways. He tried to turn again but Fargo had a hand on the dirty brown shirt, yanked the man up. The blow that whistled upward in a short arc caught the man's jaw with a sharp cracking sound and the figure flew backward in a half-somersault to hit the ground with a thud. Fargo spun around to see the flat-brimmed black hat gathering in his lariat as he spurred his horse in a circle and began to race away. He glanced at the third man, saw him half-falling onto his horse, grasping at the saddle horn, pulling himself up in stumbling haste.

The dirty brown shirt had climbed to his feet, shook his head, start to focus again. His hand went to his holster automatically as his mouth pulled back in a snarling grimace. The big Colt .45 was in Fargo's hand with a motion as quick as a rattlesnake's strike.

"I wouldn't try it, mister," he growled and the man's hand fell away from his gunbelt as his eyes saw the big barrel of the Colt aimed to blow him in two. He retreated, sidling toward his horse. "Hold it right there," Fargo said. "Let's see what the young lady wants to do with you." He glanced across at the girl. She was on one knee, rubbing her hand over the horse's legs, concentrating entirely on the animal. Fargo heard the man whirl, leap toward his horse. The man was pulling himself onto the horse and Fargo glanced at him with his lips turning inward. He

3

could blast the man out of the saddle before he got the reins up. *Stupid bastard*, he muttered silently, glanced at the girl again. She was all absorbed with examining the horse.

Fargo lowered the Colt as the man sent his horse racing off after the other two, watched him disappear into the trees. Fargo turned to the girl, not concealing his irritation. "What are you all about?" he asked. "Three men attack you and your horse and you don't even want to ask a question?"

She continued to examine the horse's legs. "I don't have to ask. I know who sent them," she said.

"You know?" Fargo frowned.

"Yes. Fred Haskell, the bastard. Or his rotten pa," she bit out, still running her fingers up and down the horse's pasterns. "Damn him. Damn the stinking, rotten bastards," she said, pulled herself to her feet, and turned to the big black-haired man. Her eyes were green, flecked with brown, he noted, and the smallish breasts had a pert, saucy upward curve to them.

"Who are you, mister?" she asked. "You're not from around here."

"Fargo," he said. "Skye Fargo. And you?"

"Liz Ryan," she said. "I owe you. Where'd you come from out of nowhere?"

"Up on the hill," he said. "Been watching you every morning."

The green eyes looked instantly sharp as they scanned the big man's face of rugged, intense strength. "Why?" she asked brusquely.

"Been waiting for a man named Ben Smith with a paymaster's wagon to arrive in Rawley," Fargo said.

"I know Ben Smith," she said.

"I missed him in Abilene and was told his next stop was out here. He's got an envelope for me. Been sleeping at the hotel in Rawley but I don't fancy hanging around towns by day so I came out here on the hill every morning and then you started showing

4

up," he told her. He left out the fact that the morning air was good for clearing the bourbon and the smell of dancehall girls out of his head.

"I guess that was lucky for Bayberry and me," Liz Ryan said, turning back to the horse, stroking its neck gently. Fargo looked at the bruises on the animal, the left foreleg tendon and cannon bone bruised, the knee with a sizable swelling. The right hind leg was lacerated along the gaskin. "Damn stinking bastards," Liz muttered.

"I guessed you were figuring on racing that horse," Fargo said and she nodded. "When?" he followed.

"Day after tomorrow," she said.

"And you figure this Fred Haskell doesn't want you to win," Fargo prodded.

"He damn sure doesn't. I'm racing against him," Liz Ryan said and the green eyes flashed. "I should've expected he'd try something like this. I should've expected," she said, berating herself.

"I take it he's not a man who can lose well," Fargo commented.

"Not this race. It's more than a race for him," she said, and Fargo saw her eyes narrow and the planes of her face seem to flatten. "If he loses, he and his rotten, land-grabbing pa have to leave my uncle and the rest of the small ranchers alone. That was my bargain or my bet, whatever you want to call it, and I held to it until he agreed."

She bit down into silence and Fargo sensed the unfinished. "And if you lose?" he asked.

Her lips bit down on each other and he saw the brown-flecked eyes grow almost sullen and she answered without looking at him. "He gets what he's been trying to get for so damn long, me in bed," she murmured.

"Sounds as though he held out for his bargain, too," Fargo said.

"I agreed because I won't lose. Bayberry can beat that damn roan of his," Liz Ryan said.

Fargo looked down at the horses' legs again. "I think you'd best withdraw for now," he said. "Let your horse's legs rest up."

She shook her head. "Can't. Withdrawing is losing. That's part of the race rules. That goes for anybody entered," she said.

"How many other horses are entered?"

"Maybe three," she said. "All plugs. It's between Fred Haskell and me. I'll race. Bayberry has a day to rest. Even off his form he can beat Fred Haskell's roan."

Fargo held back words, wondered if she were trying to convince herself or really believed in the horse. The animal wasn't all that she thought, he had decided a few days back. But there was a sense of desperation about her bet, about the tightness inside her that echoed in her eyes. He saw her turn, focus on the pinto for the first time, and her lips parted in instant admiration.

"An Ovaro. What a magnificent specimen," she said and tossed a glance at Fargo. "No horse for an ordinary cowhand," she said. "What are you, Fargo? Why are you getting a pay envelope from Ben Smith?"

"I took a silver wagon for him from Pueblo to Abilene," he told her.

"You're a Scout," she said.

"Something like that." He smiled.

"I still owe you," she said. "I'm going in to Rawley to get some of his sage and rosemary salve from Doc Atkorn for Bayberry's bruises."

"I'll ride along. Maybe Ben Smith has come in," Fargo said. He swung alongside her as she let the horse walk slowly, testing his legs. He didn't have a limp, Fargo noted. She was lucky for that.

"You going to stay around here after you pick up your pay?" she asked.

"Not likely," he answered.

"Can't say I blame you," she said.

"I don't stay anywhere for long," he said.

She drew a deep breath and the smallish breasts thrust upward firmly, a proud impudence to them. They echoed the essence of her, he decided. "This will be great country someday, maybe after it becomes a state," she said. "But now it's nothing but hardscrabble, full of drifters and gunhands and people like Blakelock Haskell, and if they don't do you in there's always the Kiowas or the Shoshoni or the Osage."

"You sound bitter. Why are you staying?" he asked.

"My uncle. He raised me and he's a good man. So are the other small homesteaders. And where else is there to go?" she said.

"Girl like you could make her way," Fargo said.

"With some drifter or dreamer? No, thanks. I want more than that, even for a short haul," she snapped as the frame buildings of Rawley came into view, the town like a thousand other towns in the territories, a collection of grubby buildings clustered around a general store, a blacksmith and stable and the dancehall. No worse but certainly no better than the others, watering holes for the lost and the wandering. He rode beside her down the single street of the town, past a big platform spring dray and a high-sided Owensboro ice wagon outside the general store. He was watching Liz Ryan as she sat the horse easily, when he saw her body stiffen and her eyes flash green fire. She was bounding from the horse instantly and he saw the man stepping from the store, tall, dark wavy hair, a young face with a hint of cruelty behind its good looks.

Two cowhands walked behind him as he left the

store and Fargo swung down from the pinto as Liz strode up to the man.

"Liz," the man exclaimed, started to grin. "Now this is a nice surprise."

"Bastard," she spit out and her hand whipped around, smashed into the man's face. "Rotten bastard," she shouted.

It was a hard, open-palmed slap and Fargo saw the man's face redden and his lips turn in, the hint of cruelty suddenly no longer a hint. "Goddamn bitch," he heard the man say, saw his arm reach out to grab at the girl's neck. The man stepped toward her and suddenly found the big black-haired man's bulk in his way.

"Easy, friend," Fargo said calmly. "The lady figures you did her a bad turn."

"Get the hell out of my way," the man said.

"Now just cool it, mister," Fargo said, keeping his voice calm. Fred Haskell's eyes took in the width of the big man's shoulders, the power latent under the folds of the shirt, and in the lake-blue eyes he caught the glint of blue shale. He stepped backward.

"She's plumb loco," he said. "I didn't do her anything."

"Three bushwhackers tried to lame her horse. I was there," Fargo said.

"Wasn't my doing," the man said. "Hell, there's a lot of betting on the race. Could be anybody wanting to cover his bets."

"It was you or your pa, Fred Haskell," Liz cut in, her eyes still full of fury. "It had your sneaking, stinking brand all over it."

"You're a yelling hellcat, as usual, Liz Ryan," the man answered. "All wild talking and nothing to back it up ever." He drew a breath, reined in his anger, and let a slow smile slide across his face and there was a cruelty in the smile, too, Fargo observed. "But we'll take you in hand after the race is over. You'll get some taming, Liz Ryan."

He turned, stalked away, but not before casting a quick glance at the big black-haired man. Fargo turned to the girl, saw the little spots of red in her cheeks as she unclenched her fists, her arms held stiffly at her sides.

"Was he right about there being plenty of betting on the race?" he asked her.

"There's always betting on any race around here," she said.

"Then it could've been somebody else sent those three after you," Fargo remarked.

"It was nobody else," she snapped back. "You can just believe that." She drew a deep breath, let the fire go out of her eyes. "Doc Atkorn's office is just down the alley here," she said. "Thanks again for helping. I still owe you," she said. "You going to stay long enough to see the race?"

"Maybe," he said. She held out her hand and he took it, strong, slender fingers that held just the right pressure to avoid being masculine.

"I'll look for you afterward if you stay," she said. She turned and went down the alleyway and he walked on, led the pinto around the rear of the houses, and came back the other side. He halted at the other end of the alleyway. She was standing with her forehead pressed against the horse's muzzle, standing head-to-head, and he heard the soft sobs. He stepped into the alleyway and she looked up, the brown-flecked eyes wet.

"You're not all that hard-nosed as you put on, are you, Liz Ryan?" he commented.

She wiped a sleeve across her eyes. "Who told you to come back?" she snapped. "Sneaking up on people." She pulled armor around herself hastily, he saw. "Go away. I'm perfectly all right," she said.

Fargo nodded. "Good," he said laconically and

9

walked on, leading the pinto behind him. He returned to Main Street, headed for the tiny bank at the center of the town, but his thoughts stayed on the proud girl that held the high fence around herself. She wasn't as all-fired sure of winning as she put on, not now, anyway. Or maybe there was so much at stake she was simply having a bout of nerves. But he was convinced of one thing. Her horse wasn't what she thought it was, even without being bruised up now. If the man, Haskell, had sent the three after the horse, he didn't deserve to win anything anywhere, Fargo muttered silently. If. It was an open question and he wondered if Haskell deserved the benefit of the doubt. The man's face held the kind of cruelty that could have ordered the attack.

He was still turning things in his mind when he reached the bank, saw Ben Smith beside the payroll wagon. The man saw him coming, waved in greeting. He had the envelope in his hand as Fargo reached him. "Sorry I couldn't wait in Abilene, Fargo," he said. "But you were a couple of days late and I had to get up here."

"No problem, Ben," Fargo said. "I can post most of this from here."

"Thanks for the job, Fargo," the man said. "I wouldn't have trusted anyone else to get through but you."

"How about a drink later? Got a few questions for you," Fargo said. "It seems you know the way of things around here."

"Sure. In an hour or so?" Ben Smith said and Fargo nodded. There was no need to talk about where. Rawley had only one place to meet for a drink and Fargo went to the hotel room and freshened up.

"Will you be checking out today?" the clerk said as he passed the front desk. Fargo began to nod, stopped himself.

"No," he said. "Not today." He went outside and

walked to the dancehall. It was a gray, lifeless place in the day, an old man slowly pushing a splint broom around the floor. Ben Smith was waiting at one of the tables with a bottle of bourbon in front of him and the big, black-haired man eased himself into a chair, taking up all of it. "Tell me about Liz Ryan. She says she knows you," he said. "And about the Haskells."

Ben Smith sat back, refreshed his drink. "Bad blood," he said. "Blakelock Haskell's an ambitious man. He's pressuring every small rancher and homesteader in the area and he's not above playing dirty. He and his son own the best land around here and they have the best herds. It's a long story to get into the details and I don't have that much time today."

"All right, tell me about this race," Fargo said.

"It's held once a year, just outside of town. This year there's a personal edge to it, but then you seem to know about that."

"A little," Fargo said. "It's an open race, I take it."

"Anybody can enter up to fifteen minutes before starting time," Ben Smith said.

"You know Fred Haskell's horse?" Fargo asked.

"No, but it ought to be a fair horse. He's got a whole corral of stock to pick from," Ben said. "You staying to watch?"

"I just might," Fargo said.

"I'll see you there," Ben said, rising. "Everybody turns out for it."

Fargo nodded, waved good-bye, and slowly finished his drink. He had another and let his thoughts turn of themselves, making their own decisions. The night came soon enough and he stayed at the dancehall for something to eat and some more bourbon. But he turned aside the girls that came to him. He'd had enough of dancehall girls and he smiled wryly to himself as one of the girls stalked off petulantly. She had a damn good shape, big breasts still holding firmness, and she was pretty enough to do without heavy

11

makeup. Yet he kept seeing a tall, lithe, narrow figure with smallish breasts, a handsome, intense face, and the dancehall girl suddenly had nothing at all to offer. He grunted, half-laughed. It wasn't all the outside equipment. It never was. Class came from inside.

He rose, went to his room, and slept. He was under the ironwood in the morning but Liz Ryan didn't show with the horse and he nodded in approval. She knew enough not to push things. He spent the day stretched out under the sun, the night in the dancehall until he went to bed.

It was easy to find the race site in the morning. He just followed a parade of wagons that headed for it. He saw a line of still more on each side of the starting place as he rode up. He'd arrived early on purpose, saw Liz beside the dark bay, adjusting the cinch buckle. Fred Haskell sat on a tall roan nearby, talking to a man with a lion's mane of gray hair, the same face as the younger man but with years on it. Blakelock Haskell wore cruelty in his face, too, but it was the cruelty of power while his son wore the cruelty of weakness. Fargo's eyes returned to the roan, swept the horse with a practiced glance. Early speed, he grunted to himself, but probably not much staying power. Yet you couldn't be certain from just one look.

He saw three other riders, dismissed the horses quickly enough, ordinary range stock. He rode the pinto around the crowd and onto the starting place, came up alongside Liz as she swung up on her horse. His eyes went to Bayberry's legs, saw that the ointment had helped, the swelling on the knee gone down. Her eyes greeted him at once.

"Hello," she said. "Glad you decided to stay. But you're supposed to be on the sidelines. Only those who're entered are allowed here."

"I know," he said blandly, watched her eyes slowly widen as the two words sank into her.

2

Her eyes finally stopped widening and she found her voice. "Why?" she blurted out.

"Figured it might be fun. Heard there was a fifty-dollar purse," he said blandly. The frown stayed, disbelief in his answer clear in the green eyes. "I get sudden ideas." He smiled, wheeled the pinto away, and felt her frown following him. He went to the side, swung from the saddle, ran his hands expertly over the horse. He was checking the cinch and the latigo hitch when he noticed the woman watching. He saw a strikingly attractive face, full red lips, firmly molded, a thin nose and wide cheeks, dark-brown hair worn softly. But it was her eyes that held him, a soft gray, like a lake on a misty morning.

She moved toward him and he took in the pale blue riding outfit, expensive written all over it, the jacket hanging open to reveal a thin white blouse underneath pressed forward by full, round breasts. The misty gray eyes grew even softer as they traveled over the pinto.

"An Ovaro. Magnificent," she breathed. She walked around the horse and the jacket moved to reveal more of the thin white blouse beneath it. The deep round breasts were tight against the thin material and he saw the dark shadows of very large, round areolas. He watched her run a hand across the pinto. "Beautifully muscled," she murmured. She moved with a soft, undulating motion and he felt the sensuousness of her along with the faint perfume she wore, a dark scent.

The misty gray eyes turned to him and fastened him with the same studied appraisal they had the pinto. "Beautifully muscled, too. You go together," she remarked, a faint smile toying with her lips. The sensuousness was very much there yet not flung at one, a whisper not a shout.

Fargo nodded, rested a hand on the pinto's rump. "I imagine if he could talk he'd have something nice to say about you," Fargo remarked.

The smile came fully to her lips, a quiet, private amusement in it. "You're new here," she said.

"Passing through," Fargo said.

"And decided to enter the race," she said and the hint of curious disbelief stayed in the soft gray eyes.

"Fifty bucks," he commented.

"You've a name, I presume," she said.

"Fargo, Skye Fargo," he answered.

"I'm Blanche Haskell," she said and the big, black-haired man's brows lifted a fraction but she caught it at once. "You know the name, I see." She half-smiled.

"I've heard talk," Fargo said blandly.

"I'm not part of Blakelock's operation. I've my own place. I'm another branch of the family. We're distant cousins," she said.

Fargo held the soft-gray eyes that had a way of insinuating more than she gave voice. "What else are you saying?" he speared.

"Don't include me in whatever you've heard," she said.

"*Racers line up*," the loud voice interrupted, calling through a megaphone.

Fargo turned, swung up onto the pinto, and looked down at Blanche Haskell. "I'll remember that," he said, wheeled away and headed for the crude starting line. A very compelling woman, he reflected, perhaps thirty, not more. Her sensuousness stayed with him as did the dark scent of her perfume. Worth further investigating, he grunted to himself. She sent out signals. But only to those who could pick up on them. He shook off further thoughts of Blanche Haskell as he reached the starting line, guided the pinto to one end of the group. He made the sixth horse and he saw Liz Ryan at the other end of the line. Her handsome, angular face wore tenseness. Fred Haskell sat his roan beside her but her eyes stared straight ahead.

Fargo gathered the reins in hand, shifted slightly forward in the saddle, dismissed the other three horses again with a quick glance. The course was a straight run for the first quarter-mile, he saw, with flags marking the rest of the turns. The starter climbed atop a barrel and raised the magaphone to his lips. "Twice around the course, remember," the man called out, then lifted the pistol into the air. Fargo half-rose in the saddle and let the shot crack the air, watched Fred Haskell's roan break first with the initial speed he'd expected.

He sent the pinto out fast but not too fast, holding back with the three range horses. He saw Liz Ryan matching the roan stride for stride as both horses swung into the lead. He grunted disapprovingly. She was letting herself be sucked into a mistake. The onlookers were whooping and hollering as the horses thundered down the straightaway past them and Fargo let the pinto have a little more head, quickly pulled up almost abreast of Fred Haskell and Liz. He saw her throw a quick glance over at him and hoped she'd see to fall off and save her horse. But she continued to match Fred Haskell's roan and Fargo shook his head. He stayed a half-length back of the roan and saw Fred Haskell glance at him, the man's thin mouth set in a hard line, his wavy hair flattened out by the wind. He held back again, let the roan and Liz Ryan's Bayberry open a length on him as the first turn came up. A water jump lay a dozen yards after the turn and

15

he watched Liz let her horse take the jump at full speed, the quarterhorse muscle structure pulling itself up and over with a raw power.

She gained a head lead on the jump, he saw, and watched Haskell's roan make it up as soon as they were on the ground again. Another jump appeared, a hedgerow, and once again Liz made up time as she let the bay power over the obstacle. Fargo dropped back a little, let the pinto take the jump with deliberate ease. Fred Haskell had pulled a head in front of Liz again and Fargo let the pinto go for a few moments, closed the distance at once, pulled up alongside Liz Ryan, eased slightly ahead of her, and saw the concern touch her face. He stayed for a moment, then dropped back, glanced at her, again hoped she get the message. But she continued to push the bay at the roan, staying almost stride for stride.

Fargo uttered a silent curse at her. It was plain she was afraid to let Fred Haskell open up too much distance but she was using up her horse fast, going on that confidence in her horse which was unjustified. The last jump was a high stake fence and once again Fargo watched her let the bay power over it, saw the horse come down heavy, and his lips drew back. The bay was already tiring. Fargo took the jump with smooth ease and caught up to Liz again as they rounded the turn and headed back down the straightaway past the double line of onlookers. Haskell on the roan stayed a full length in front. The other three range riders had fallen far behind.

Liz, flinging an angry glance at Fargo, pushed the bay again and Fargo dropped back a head and watched her continue to push her horse. He heard the cheers of the onlookers as they went down the straight section of the course, the sound carried away by the wind almost as quickly as it reached his ears. He went into the first curve again, holding just back of Liz Ryan.

The bay went over the water jump but this time he took it low and Fargo saw the horse starting to shorten stride, a sure sign of weariness. The roan had opened up a little more than a length now but was starting to tire also, Fargo noted.

When they reached the hedgerow jump, the roan was two full lengths ahead. Fargo let the pinto go and the magnificently muscled black-and-white horse closed distance with the sheer joy of power and speed. He came abreast of Liz, held back, and saw her start to push Bayberry again, the horse laboring, now. Fargo grimaced and moved ahead. She was done, her horse spent, her only chance hanging on the roan doing a real fade by the last jump. But he couldn't risk that. He let the pinto move, come alongside Fred Haskell as the stake fence jump came into view.

He enjoyed the surprise in Haskell's face, saw the anger wipe away the surprise as the man went to the whip. Fargo was surprised to see the roan still had speed left and the horse shot forward. Haskell let the horse drift to the right as they neared the jump. He continued to send the roan to the right and Fargo saw he intended a bump just before the jump. Fargo let him come over further, less than an inch away now, then veered the pinto to the right, also, took the jump at an angle, sailing high over the top of the fence. He saw the roan follow, going straight on at the jump, just clearing it.

The pinto hit the ground, started to go full out. Once again in surprise, Fargo saw the roan coming at him. The horse had speed and stamina, more than it appeared to have, and Haskell drew alongside. The man was whipping hard, bent low in the saddle as they turned into the straightaway, the finish line looming ahead. Haskell let the roan swing in close again, brought the whip down in a wide arc and the tip of it grazed the pinto's neck.

Fargo pulled back on the reins to prevent the pinto from veering away, breaking stride. But he had lost precious split-seconds as the roan pulled straight on. He decided to risk another half-second loss, moved to the right, away from Haskell. The finish line was too close now and Fargo brought his hand down on the pinto's rump, a sharp slap, hardly hard, but the horse responded instantly. The black-and-white form hurtled forward, roaring past Haskell's roan as though it were standing still to cross the finish line a head in front.

Fargo heard the cheers hang in the air as he slowed the pinto to a trot, turned, headed back between the cheering spectators. Liz had finished a poor third, he saw, and he let the pinto move from a trot to a walk, blow out wind, cool down, and finally he halted before the finishing line and swung down from the saddle. A man came forward to hand him an envelope with the fifty dollars in it, shake his hand, and admire the pinto. Fargo saw Fred Haskell ride up, his horse snorting heavily, jump down from the saddle to face him, his handsome face dark with fury.

"Who the hell are you, mister?" the man demanded.

"Fargo," he was answered.

"Why'd you enter the damn race?" Fred Haskell roared. "Liz Ryan put you up to it?"

Fargo saw Liz Ryan dismounting nearby, watching Fred Haskell's rage. "No," he said. "I just didn't figure you ought to win."

He saw Fred Haskell's thin mouth grow thinner, the rage in his eyes made of hate. "I won't be forgetting this, mister," the man snarled.

"I imagine not," Fargo said calmly and watched Fred Haskell whirl, stalk off. Fargo turned, went over to where Liz Ryan stood watching, one hand on the bay's neck.

"You're off the hook," he said.

"I didn't ask you to take me off the hook," she said angrily, the brown-flecked eyes a dark green. "I could have won," she said. He saw pride and uncertainty rising up inside her.

"Why didn't you, then?" he asked coldly. "You didn't make second."

She winced but only in her eyes. "With just him to worry about I'd have run a different race," she said.

"You're lying to yourself and you know it," Fargo threw back at her. "You didn't have the horse to win, even if you hadn't run a dumb race." She blinked and her lips tightened but she kept her chin high. "You better be more grateful or I'll call in my claim," Fargo said.

"What claim?" She frowned instantly.

"You were going to go to bed with the winner and I won," he said blandly, saw her mouth fall open as he turned and strode away, leading the pinto behind him. He saw the tall, pale-blue figure on the sidelines, watching, a small smile curling the full lips. Beside her, he saw the gray-maned head of Blakelock Haskell, the man no taller than the woman but his figure burly, his face the face of a man used to giving orders and being obeyed. Fargo halted before the young woman.

"I see you know Liz Ryan," she said.

"A little," Fargo said.

"Real spitfire, that one," Blakelock Haskell cut in and Fargo turned to the man, saw he had sharp blue eyes and again noted the hint of cruelty in the large face, but that of power, not weakness.

"My cousin, Blakelock Haskell," Blanche introduced.

The man produced a magnanimous smile. "Fine race and a fine horse. It'll do my son good to lose for a change," he said. Fargo nodded quietly.

19

"Cousin Blakelock tells me you're something of a legend," Fargo heard Blanche say.

Fargo shrugged. "People talk. They make a name for a man."

"You've made your own name, I hear," the woman insisted.

"I first heard about Fargo down Texas way," the man said. "The Trailsman, he was called. The very best there is." Fargo saw Blanche's soft-gray eyes appraising him again, with renewed interest. Blakelock Haskell's voice broke in again. "How about coming to the ranch for dinner tonight?" the man said. "Man wins a good race he deserves a good dinner."

Fargo's eyes went to Blanche. She half-nodded to him. "I'll be there if you'll come," she said and the gray eyes were insinuating again.

"Why not?" Fargo agreed. "Much obliged."

"At seven, then," Blakelock Haskell said and strode away. Fargo walked beside the young woman until she halted at a small cart, a Basket Phaeton with its big rear wheels, smaller front ones, and graceful, delicate lines.

"More a town cart," he commented and she shrugged.

"Yes, but I prefer it to a buckboard. More elegance," she answered and he had to agree. He watched her climb into the slender cart, a high step and the slit in her riding skirt revealed a long, shapely calf. "You will be there this evening," she said, questioning suddenly.

"Definitely. You're counting on it," Fargo said, catching her off-balance and her lips parted for a moment. But she recovered quickly, taking the reins up, giving him a too-sweet smile.

"A touch of presumption, isn't that?" she said.

"A touch of knowing," Fargo returned.

The gray-mist eyes held steady. "You could be wrong."

"I could be," he said slowly. "But I'm not."

She touched the reins to the horse, drove unhurriedly away, not looking back, and Fargo smiled after her. He swung onto the pinto and thought about the misted invitations in her eyes, promises offered yet not offered. Blanche Haskell would make the evening worthwhile. A beautiful woman always helped make an evening.

He rode slowly from town. It was a little early and he'd time to spare. He was ambling the pinto across a tree-studded field when he saw the figure riding toward him, the light-brown hair swinging from side to side, glinting copper highlights in the afternoon sun. She halted before him, met his eyes with something between defiance and guilt.

"You come to be grateful?" he asked.

Her eyes flared at once. "Not the way you're thinking," she snapped. He made no comment and she drew a deep breath that made the smallish breasts stand out with saucy boldness under her shirt. "I know you tried to help me out and I'm beholden to you for the thought," she said.

"Tried?" he asked blandly.

"All right, more than tried. You took me off the hook, in your words," she said.

"In anybody's words," he cut in.

She glared in a moment of exasperation. "Dammit, you have to make it difficult?" she snapped.

"Just want to keep the record straight," Fargo said. "You're trying to slide the truth around."

"All right, you took me off the hook. Maybe I wouldn't have won," she said and ignored the glance he gave her. "But you took Fred Haskell and his pa off the hook, too. Everything's back the way it was before the race and that's pretty damn bad," she said, her face clouding. "My Uncle Barney wants to see you. He was talking to Ben Smith about you after I told him how you helped me with those three who tried to lame Bayberry. Will you come talk to him?"

Fargo gave a wry grunt. "Suddenly I'm the belle of the ball around here?" he said.

"Blakelock Haskell ask you to come see him?" Liz Ryan asked.

"Tonight," Fargo nodded.

"I figured he might when I saw him talking to you. She was eyeing you pretty damn sweetly, too," the girl said.

"Blanche Haskell?" Fargo said. "I hear she's not into her cousin's operation. In fact they're not even close, I'm told."

"Skunks are skunks, no matter what part of the family tree they come from." Liz Ryan sniffed.

Fargo gave her a slow smile. "There wouldn't be a little plain old-fashioned female jealousy in that, would there?" he asked.

"Jealousy?" she flared, too quickly, green eyes sparking fire. "Why would I be jealous of her?"

"She's well turned out, damn good-looking, and has a fine figure. That's usually reason enough," Fargo said mildly.

"It's not for me and I don't think she's got such a fine figure," the girl flung back, started to wheel her horse around. "Are you going to come see my Uncle Barney?" she snapped.

"Tomorrow afternoon. Where?" Fargo said.

"I'll come get you," Liz Ryan said, slapped the bay on the rump, and rode off at a fast canter.

"Glad you're not the jealous type," Fargo called after her. She didn't look back but he saw the horse move into a faster pace and he laughed. Turning the pinto, he headed back to the hotel, went to his room and shed clothes, washed with cool water out of a big,

22

ceramic basin, lay down for an hour naked, rested his muscles from the hard riding of the race.

He was dressed in a fresh change of clothes and after asking directions to the Haskell ranch, rode out onto the flat land west of Rawley, finally came to the low, widely spaced corrals and buildings of the spread. The name *HASKELL* was carved into a curved pair of longhorns over the entranceway and he rode leisurely to the ranchhouse, tied the pinto to the hitching rail outside. He paused to glance at the corral full of whiteface cattle, a good, well-fed herd. He lifted the iron door-knocker and a few moments later was admitted by an elderly black man wearing a slightly frayed black frock coat. The man took his hat, waited politely, and Fargo gave him the big Colt .45, watched him put it atop a tall rack along with his hat.

Shown into a large living room, he saw Blanche Haskell at the end of a long sofa as Blakelock Haskell rose to greet him. The tall, wavy-haired figure of Fred Haskell rose from a leather chair and Fargo saw his handsome face darken at once. The young man shot a glance at his father.

"What's he doing here?" he barked.

"Fargo's my dinner guest," Blakelock Haskell answered.

"Damn, you didn't tell me about this," Fred Haskell protested angrily.

"Didn't see any need to," his father said calmly.

Fred Haskell's eyes went to the big, black-haired man, sullen anger in their dark orbs. "Then you can count me out, I'm particular who I eat with," he rasped, started to move from the room.

"Fred," Blakelock Haskell called out sternly but the younger man was already striding across the room. Fargo saw he was thinking about banging into him, smiled inwardly as he saw Fred Haskell change his mind and brush past him and storm out the door.

"My apologies," Blakelock Haskell said smoothly to Fargo. "Fred's always been headstrong. He can't stand losing at anything."

"Family trait, I'd guess," Fargo said and let a smile take the edge from the comment.

Blakelock Haskell returned the smile. "Yes, I suppose it is. But years teach us how to handle ourselves better." He turned toward a dark wood cabinet. "Bourbon?"

Fargo nodded, let his eyes find Blanche Haskell again. She held a glass in her hand, the mist-gray eyes faintly amused. A midnight-blue skirt set off a white blouse that was cut square and low at the neck. It let her cream-white breasts rise over the top of the neckline, tantalizingly beautiful mounds. "Approve?" she asked, reading his eyes easily.

"Definitely," Fargo said, took the bourbon Blakelock Haskell brought him, and sat down beside Blanche, let his eyes scan the room. Tastefully furnished, good solid furniture, mostly pine and cedar pieces, a big breakfront against one wall holding sturdy earthenware dishes. Low cross-beams stood out against the white stucco of the roof. His nostrils picked up the faint scent of Blanche's perfume, different from the one she'd worn in the morning, a gardenia scent. She moved slightly, let her shoulder brush his, and he felt the soft smoothness of her.

"Blakelock had the cook make beef curry tonight," she said. "My favorite dish."

"In honor of Blanche's visit," the man said. "Seeing as how she seldom comes to see us."

Fargo turned his eyes on the woman, the question in them, and she half-laughed as she sipped her bourbon. "Blakelock and I disagree on so many things," she said. "But I promised not to argue with him tonight in front of his guest."

"Don't let me stop you," Fargo said.

"No, this is Blakelock's evening. I'll not interfere," she said with quiet amusement. The sensuousness of her was more than in the mist-gray eyes, Fargo decided, a banked-fire quality that she exuded without conscious effort. The cook appeared, a small, leathery-faced Oriental, wheeling in a tray of food, and Blakelock led the way to the large, uncovered oak table in the adjoining room, set with the earthenware dishes and heavy glass goblets. They sat at one end of the long table, Fargo across from Blanche, Haskell at the head. The curried beef was excellent, made more so by too much trail food and hotel fare. A large picture window faced Fargo and he could look out across much of the corral area and the fields beyond. Even in the dim moonlight it was an impressive piece of land.

"How many acres do you have?" he asked Haskell.

"Some five hundred acres," the man said. "Started out with a few acres, worked it, got some good steers and hired some hands to help me. It grew fast because I was alert to opportunities." He poured Fargo's goblet full with water from a heavy crystal pitcher. "A lot of people resent a man who takes advantage of opportunities."

"Such as the other small ranchers around here," Fargo said, pushing away from his emptied plate and drawing on his bourbon.

"That's right," Blakelock Haskell said with sudden vehemence. "That's what I want to tell you about." He paused, glanced at Blanche, and Fargo followed his eyes, saw her faintly amused smile as she toyed with her glass. "Blanche doesn't approve of what I'm going to tell you. She thinks I'm being presumptious," he said.

25

"Seems to me I've heard that word before," Fargo remarked and enjoyed Blanche Haskell's little laugh, a low, throaty, sexy sound. He returned his glance to Haskell. "I'm listening," he said.

The man rose, went to the window, gestured outside it with a sweep of his hand. "All that land out there, it needs strength, money, and something else to use it right. It needs vision, a man who understands the whole picture. If this territory is ever going to amount to anything it'll take men who think big, not small."

"Everybody starts small. You told me you did, too," Fargo said.

"Hell, yes, but I didn't ever think small. There's a big difference between starting small and thinking small," the man said. "Now you take those ranchers that keep bad-mouthing me, they're happy with their little spreads. They're small and they think small. Even their big plans have small ends. They're lice, grubbers all of them."

"Might be so, but it seems to me that this country's been built out of small people making their own way for themselves," Fargo said mildly.

"No more. The territory will be better off without their kind. It needs big thinking and big doing," Haskell reiterated.

Fargo felt Blanche Haskell's eyes on him, turned to the amused smile toying with her lips. "Ask him, Fargo, you're thinking about it," she said, the throaty little laugh in her words.

He allowed her a smile. She was good at reading faces. Or perhaps just catching the obvious. "I have been wondering," he admitted, turning back to Blakelock Haskell. "Why are you bothering to tell me all this?" he queried.

The man's gray-mane head tilted to one side and he seemed to think for a moment, his lips pursing. "A man with your reputation comes to town and people get all kinds of ideas," he said after a moment. "Liz Ryan's uncle has some wild plans, I've heard. He might look you up with an offer. It just seemed to me you ought to know the facts about the kind of people you'd be dealing with before you waste your time on them. Chicken-scratch people, that's what they are, all of them," he said.

"I'll keep that in mind," Fargo said blandly. It was obvious that Blakelock Haskell was concerned over whatever the small ranchers had in mind. "I'm not here to pick up jobs," he told the man honestly.

"Glad to hear that," the man said warmly. "I've tried to help those people, made 'em damn good propositions and offers. Lord knows, I've tried," he said, shaking his head.

"Enough of this," Blanche intruded and turned the rest of the evening to lighter subjects until finally she leaned back, yawned. "It's time for me to head home," she announced. "It's a long enough drive at any hour and especially at night." She gave Fargo a direct stare, brows faintly lifted. "I was hoping you might see me back to my place. I don't like driving alone at night."

"Wouldn't do anything else," he said.

Blanche rose, waited for the elderly manservant to bring her wool shawl which she arranged around her shoulders. "I'll get my carriage and meet you outside," she said to Fargo. Turning to Blakelock, her eyes laughed again. "See, I didn't argue at all with you," she teased.

The man spoke to Fargo: "Blanche doesn't agree with my pressing the small ranchers. She feels they'll all fall by the wayside themselves," he said.

"What will be, will be. Blakelock can't accept that," she countered. "My dear cousin's too impatient." She flicked a glance at Fargo, whirled away, and disappeared out the door.

"Come by again if you're staying around," the man said to Fargo. "Might you be visiting a spell?"

"Not likely," Fargo replied. "But thanks for dinner. And your view of things," he added. The elderly black man appeared with his Colt and hat and Fargo holstered the gun, went outside, and swung up onto the pinto. His thoughts hung on the evening's talk as he waited for Blanche to appear. On the surface it had been an evening of friendly conversation. On the surface, he grunted silently. The drive and power of Blakelock Haskell hadn't been concealed. That was impossible, anyway. Had it all been only a smooth performance, he wondered. Had Blakelock Haskell given greed and aggression the face of reasonableness and sincere conviction?

The shallow Basket Phaeton rolled out of the nearby barn and he put the thoughts aside, swung in beside the little cart. Blanche drove at a brisk pace and they moved along narrow roads and cut across fields only dimly lighted by a shallow moon.

"What do you do out here all by yourself?" Fargo asked. "You raise your own stock?"

"No. I raise different kinds of crops under controlled conditions to see which ones will do best in the soil out here. Sort of an experimental ranch," she said. "I also cross-breed different strains of some crops. My pa left me with a good bit of money and I like to experiment."

"Just with crops?" Fargo smiled.

The low, throaty laugh hung for a moment in the night air. "I like to see things grow," she said as a small group of houses appeared and she steered the wagon toward them. Fargo saw the rows of neatly planted crops extending back of a modest ranchhouse and beyond the house two outbuildings, one with a light in the window. "I've three men who work in the fields. That's their bunkhouse," she explained, halting the wagon and swinging down to the ground as Fargo dismounted. She went into the house, not bothering to ask if he'd like to come in, her way one which said she simply expected him to do so. He followed her into the house and she turned on a lamp which gave enough light for him to see a richly furnished room, a Persian carpet on the floor and rich amber drapes on the windows, a long open-faced breakfront filled with porcelains and Wedgewood china.

"Experimenting with crops must pay off," he commented.

"It will," she said, whisking the scarf from her shoulders. "But all this is inherited." She went to a wooden liquor cabinet and poured two bourbons, handed him one as she sat down on a long, deep-brown sofa, and Fargo watched how her full breasts pushed up over the edge of the neckline.

"How did you enjoy your evening with Cousin Blakelock, Fargo?" she asked, the amusement in her mist-gray eyes.

"Fine. I just can't decide whether he was giving me friendly advice or a warning," Fargo said.

"Some of both, maybe," Blanche Haskell said. "He can be quite unpleasant when he's crossed but I wouldn't like to see him tangle with you." Fargo nodded at the backhanded compliment. "You're not the ordinary kind," she said. "I sympathize with Blakelock even when I disagree with his methods. He can make so many mistakes in judgment."

Fargo sat down beside her, drained his bourbon. "How about you?" he asked. "You make mistakes in judgment, too?"

The mist-gray eyes simmered. "Never," she said, leaned forward, and he met her halfway, closed his mouth over hers. He felt her tremble, surprised at the reaction, and then she drew away. The gray eyes held no toying amusement now, almost a kind of alarm instead. He pressed his mouth to hers again, worked her lips open and tasted the warm wetness of her tongue and her gasp was shuddered. Her arms slid around his neck and she held tight as he let his tongue probe, slowly first, in a tantalizing circle. He felt her own tongue respond, slipping forward to meet his, explore, taste, ask. His hand pressed down over one creamy mound, pushing the neckline of the dress down, and he felt her reach up, fingers finding a snap and the front of the dress came open. He drew back to gaze at the full beauty of her breasts, soft-cream, very rounded, almost as full at the top as at the undersides and the brown-pink areolas exceptionally large, like small saucers around the pink nipples that were already starting to rise. He touched them with his thumb, a brief, fleeting touch.

"Oh, God, ohhhh . . ." she breathed. "Aaaauuuuhh-hh . . ." The deep cry seemed to rise from some hidden place and her arms pulled him down to bury his face into her breasts. He took one full mound into his mouth, let his tongue trace a slow circle around the edges of the areola, and she cried out and he felt her hands pushing at her skirt, unclasping and tugging, and suddenly her naked legs were flailing against him. He shed clothes without taking his mouth from her breast and when he pressed his hardness against her abdomen she screamed.

"Jesus, Fargo, oh, Jesus, give me, give me, oh, please, please," she gasped at him and he let his hands move down across her hips slowly, tracing an erratic pathway down through the wiry triangle, not too thick at all, then halting, and she gasped out entreaties again. Her hand shot out to find his, thrust it between her thighs. "Please, please, Jesus, please." He let his fingers

30

touch only, felt the streaming juices of her, and she screamed again. "Yes, oh, yes, please."

He pressed his hand to her and felt the soft wet lips open at once, the portal waiting, throbbing, and she was making little whimpering sounds. He rose over her, let his swollen maleness slide into her. "Aaaaiiiiii . . . oh, Jesus," she screamed. "Oh, God, oh, yes, yes." She pushed up for him and he felt himself pulled deeper. Her legs clamped tight around him and her stomach sucked in and out and she cried out, a rasping sound in rhythm with each motion. The sound grew louder, deep, began to be little half-screams. He felt her tighten, the wet, warm funnel constricting around him, and then she was almost leaping under him and the half-screams turned into a long, howling cry. He came with her, furiously, and she held to him, matching his every plunging thrust until suddenly she flung herself backward, arching up and holding in a shuddered cry, then, abruptly, falling back to lie as if lifeless on the Persian rug.

He held a moment, then started to slide out of her, and she snapped into life, grasping at him. "No." She coughed. "No, stay with me." She pulled at him, tried to close her thighs but they fell open at the effort and she moaned softly. He stayed atop her, his face buried into the softness of the full breasts until, finally, his lusting organ diminished, he fell from her, and she turned to cradle herself in his arms.

The wild fire had flamed and died away with an overwhelming power and she was the first to sit up, pull herself onto her elbows, pushing back her hair. The mist-gray eyes were on him as he sat up, fulfilled and questioning. "It's been a long, dry spell, hasn't it?" he said softly.

She nodded, half-closed her eyes. "Too long," she murmured. "When I first saw you I knew that too long had to come to an end. But I was afraid of one

31

thing." He told her to continue with his eyes. "I didn't want you to think it had anything to do with Blakelock, that I might be playing up to you for his sake."

"I knew better than that," he told her.

The mist-gray eyes studied him. "How?" she questioned.

"Reading signs," he said. "That's what I do best. That's why I'm called the Trailsman. I know a trail when I come onto one, whether it's possum or pussy."

The hint of a smile touched her lips. "Yes, I'd say there's no doubt about that," she said.

He cupped one deep, large breast in his hand and she pressed hard against his palm. "Why so long a dry spell?" he asked.

"Nobody around that excited me," she answered. "I got involved in other things, my work. Channeling energies, they call it. One can do it, until someone like you comes along."

"Then you remember, is that it?" he said.

"Then you try to make up for yesterdays and store up for tomorrows," she said. She pulled from his grasp, slid herself downward, and her mouth came onto his abdomen, moved down, traced a quick pathway to the symbol of her wanting. He felt her lips come open, curl around him, gently at first. He gave a little groan of pleasure at the enveloping warmth of her mouth. "I told you I like to see things grow," she said, the low, throaty laugh in the murmured words, and she proceeded to prove it, sweet pullings and soft-tongued caresses, bringing him to pulsating strength again, her little sounds of pure delight accompanying the transformation. When she paused, drawing in deep breaths of pleasure, he turned her over, moved into the fleshy gates she opened at once for him and once again she exploded in frenzy, wanting and needing melting into a rage of pleasure.

He didn't hold himself back, saw that she was reaching that moment of moments with frenzied speed. He was ready, exploding with her as once again her body arched up and backward, lifting him with her, and the scream of pure ecstacy filled the room.

She held, quivering, and then again seemed to go lifeless, falling back heavily onto the thickness of the rug to lay hardly breathing, her eyes closed. But this time he stayed in her until, finally, he fell away and she groaned, moved to lay beside him. She slept and he catnapped with her till it was almost dawn. He moved from her, began to dress, and she opened her eyes, focused on him as he pulled on trousers. "Your hands will be turning out soon. I think I'd best be on my way," he said. He enjoyed the beauty of her as he dressed, deep breasts falling slightly to the sides, the saddle of her wide hips, her thighs full and soft and lying slightly apart, a thoroughly sensual body. She lay quiet, the mist-gray eyes watching him enjoy her, sat up only when he'd finished dressing.

"Will you come back tonight?" she asked, swinging up to sit at the edge of the sofa.

"Can't say for sure," he told her, remembering the promise he'd made Liz Ryan.

"Tomorrow?" she asked.

He nodded. "By then," he said.

Her eyes studied him. "Ever think of staying in one place?" she asked, saw the smile touch the corners of his mouth. "You've heard the question before, I take it," she said. He nodded. "There's always a first time for saying yes," she said.

"Maybe," he allowed. "But this isn't it. Got too many things still unfinished."

She rose, slid arms around him, kissed him, her lips wet and soft. "Don't get involved with anything but me while you're here." she said.

"Wouldn't think of it." He grinned, the answer

more true than not. He slipped from the door and left. He was riding into Rawley as the new day began to slip over the tops of the distant hills. In his room at the hotel he pulled down the window shade, undressed, and fell into bed, the smell of Blanche Haskell still on him, the dark perfume of her and woman smell of her, all mingled together, clinging, a good smell. He thought about her as sleep nudged at him. No ordinary wanton. A mind, an independent spirit behind the sensuousness. He pondered idly about her relationship with Blakelock Haskell. Distantly cordial, it seemed. Disapproving yet not without sympathy. But she'd said that much herself with disarming honesty. Fargo turned on his side. He always enjoyed a complex woman. He smiled as he closed his eyes. They brought an added dimension with them, in and out of bed.

He fell asleep as the sun came up on the other side of the window shade.

3

It was late when he woke and he stretched, slowly rose, and washed, Blanche Haskell in his thoughts as he relived the pleasures of the evening in his mind. He dressed, strapped on the gunbelt, and adjusted the hang of the holster with the big Colt, one of the few .45 caliber Army models made. He went outside, blinked in the brightness of the afternoon sun, and made his way to the dancehall where he bought a cup of coffee from the kitchen attendant. He sipped it in the dimness of the main room with the tables pushed back for the floor to be mopped. He finished only half, drew his lips back at the bitter taste of the old coffee grounds, and went back outside. He had started to stroll toward the hotel when Fred Haskell crossed in front of him, halted to block his path. The younger man's handsomeness was marred by the cruel line of his mouth, a line that became a tight-lipped snarl.

"You hanging around to cause more trouble?" Fred Haskell slid out.

"Not unless you figure to start some," Fargo said casually.

"I got some advice for you, mister," Fred Haskell said. "Get your ass out of here and quick."

"If you're not careful, you'll make me think you don't like me," Fargo said blandly.

Fred Haskell's mouth grew thinner until it seemed to almost disappear as his lips pressed hard on each other. "I warned you, mister," he bit out, whirled on his heel, and strode away. He'd gone halfway down the street when Fargo saw the three men step from one side to fall in behind him. One, the shortest of the trio, wore a dirty yellow shirt, he noted, and his eyes followed Fred Haskell until the man reached his horse and rode away with his friends. Fred Haskell was trouble, Fargo grunted to himself, nasty and vengeful and used to getting whatever he wanted, one way or another. Like father like son, he wondered, one smooth, the other rough? Blanche was definitely a different branch of the family.

He strolled back to the hotel, leaned against the hitching post, and waited. He waited for longer than he wanted to wait, was growing irritated and impatient when he spied Liz Ryan riding toward him on the bay. She came to a halt before him as he leaned against the edge of the hotel post. Her brown-flecked eyes held something in them, a kind of hostile haughtiness that made him wonder, but he let his glance take in the handsomeness of her high-planed face, the brown hair with coppery glints. She wore a jonquil blouse, the smallish breasts turned up impudently to form two sharp little points against the thin material. He found himself thinking about Blanche Haskell. The two women were so different. Form follows function. Perhaps personality follows body, he speculated. Blanche Haskell was dark wine; Liz Ryan pepper and spice.

"You're late," he growled.

"I'm here." She shrugged. "You coming?" He straightened, untied the pinto, and climbed into the saddle. She rode out of town at once and he drew up alongside her as they rode across a field of wild bergamot.

"Something special eating you today?" he asked.

Her glance was quick and sharp. "Nothing that's your concern. Not yet," she said.

"Whatever the hell that means," he muttered. A thought flickered in his mind and he tossed it out. "You want I should call off meeting your uncle?" he said.

He saw the flash of alarm touch her face for an instant. "No," she said. "No."

"No, but what?" he pressed.

He saw the glint of resentment come into the green eyes again. "We'll see," was all she'd say and he shrugged, rode along with her as she broke into a canter to go up a low rise and down the other side. Dusk was starting to purple the sky as they came to her place and Fargo swept the layout with a long glance, seeing all the little things that revealed so much to the experienced eye, a herd of almost too-thin steers in a modest corral, barns in need of paint, fence posts that should have been replaced. The main house was in good condition, modest in size but with a stone foundation.

36

The man came out of the house as they rode up, was standing with hand outstretched as Fargo dismounted. He had reddish hair, a pair of bright blue eyes in a square-jawed face that echoed Ireland all over it. "My uncle Barney McCall," Liz introduced. The man's grip was powerful, his smile expansive.

"Glad you could come see us, Fargo," Barney McCall said. He gestured toward the corrals. "Nothing like where you were last night," he said. "Liz told me Blakelock Haskell had you over."

"He did," Fargo said as he followed the man inside, found himself in a worn but comfortable living room with an ox-cart-wheel chandelier. The man poured him a glass of whiskey. "Kentucky rye," he said and Fargo felt the hotness of it in his throat.

"I don't imagine Blakelock Haskell had anything good to say about any of us," Barney McCall commented, his eyes hardening.

"Not that I can remember," Fargo said mildly, met Liz's eyes for a moment. She had a held-back air about her.

"He's been trying to swallow us all up for years," she said.

"He and that no-good son of his are plain rotten, thieving, murdering bastards," Barney McCall said.

"Strong words," Fargo commented. "He allowed to me that he's tried to help you people, made you good offers."

The man gave a derisive, snorting noise. "If help means trying to squeeze you out of existence, offering you next to nothing for your land, and then trying to force you off it when you hold out," he said. "If help means murdering and burning and terrorizing folks into running, then taking over their lands, well, then, I guess he's been helping us."

"The Olsons chased Fred Haskell off their land one day," Liz said. "Gave him a beating, too. By the next week they were all murdered, ambushed on their way to Sunday prayer meeting. Sid and Patty Hanz refused to let him hog their water with his herd and they were burned out soon after. They up and left. Plenty of others have been terrorized and finally just gave up and ran."

"But you can't prove it was the Haskells, I take it," Fargo said.

"Proving's one thing. Knowing's another," she answered.

"Let's back up a bit. How has he been squeezing you all out of business?" Fargo asked.

Barney McCall drained his drink, sat back in his chair. "First, you've got to understand how it was around here. He always drove his herds down to Abilene in Texas twice a year to sell his beef for the best prices. He's got the hands to make a hard drive like that. We never did so we sold to the small, local buyers nearby. First thing he did was to get control of those buyers and next thing we knew they wouldn't buy from us."

Fargo frowned, thought back of how Blakelock Haskell had put it. "I was told he offered to let you include your stock in his drives to Abilene and sell them for you," he said.

"Oh, he did that. He's a smooth one. It made him look like the big man helping us little folk. But you know what he paid us for that? Half the market price for our stock. He kept the rest as his fee for driving our herds with his," Barney said with undisguised bitterness.

"Half, mind you, fifty percent," Liz cut in angrily. "The going rate for driving somebody else's cattle with yours is a ten-percent fee."

"He figured that would drive us out of business. Half the market price hardly covered feed costs for our herds. But we all managed to hang in, cut back on feed, and kept raising new stock. That's when the murdering and burning began and now he thinks he was us once and for all with his last move."

"What was that?" Fargo asked.

"He told us if he drives our herds with his this time we'll only get a third of the market price," the man said. "A third, damn his rotten hide."

"He knows we can't live on a third of the market price," Liz said. "And we can't get anything better nearby because he's seen to that and none of us have the hands to make a long drive south alone. We'll have to sell out, he figures."

Fargo's eyes narrowed in thought. The picture was hardly the one Blakelock Haskell had painted. The man was clever as well as smooth and apparently equally ruthless. He had Barney McCall and the others pretty much where he wanted them, it seemed.

"I'd say you're in a box canyon," Fargo remarked.

"Almost but not yet. We've one chance and we've decided to take it. We're going to all put our herds together and make our own drive south. But not to Abilene. We've heard their paying twice as much for good beef stock in New Mexico. We've put all our spare cash together, all of us, and made enough to pay you."

Fargo frowned. "Pay me? For what?" he asked.

"To lead the drive. We need someone like you for that," the man said. "We can make it if we have a real fine trailsman. When I heard about you and here you were right in town, I went to the others right away. They all agreed on it."

"You're loco." Fargo frowned back. "You'd need a lot more than me. You'd need range hands, good ones experienced at handling cattle, and enough of them. You said you didn't have the hands to make a drive like that."

"We've decided we have them by pooling all our

39

people together. Everybody's just going to have to take off and pitch in," Barney McCall said.

Fargo's frown stayed. They were being carried away with desperation and enthusiasm. "You think Haskell will just stand by and let you do this all nice and peaceful?" he asked. "Not if he's the kind of man you've said he is."

"Maybe not but he'll find out there's not much he can do about it to stop us," Barney said confidently.

"I think you'll find out there's a hell of a lot he can do," Fargo said. "And if he doesn't, going down New Mexico way is going into Apache country. That ought to be enough for you to call off the whole idea."

Liz answered, her voice crisp. "We can't call if off. It's our last chance. If we make it, we'll all have more than enough to last the winter and raise our young stock. But most important, we'll have enough to stop Blakelock Haskell from driving us from our lands."

"And if you don't make it?" Fargo pressed.

"We're done in anyway," Barney said. "We've no choice but to go on with it. But we know our chances would be a thousand percent better with you leading the drive, Fargo. We've got five hundred dollars now and you'll get another five hundred when we sell off in New Mexico."

Fargo didn't answer, his lips tightened as the lake-blue eyes stared out into space. "That's good money, man," he heard Barney McCall say.

"It's not the money, that's fine," Fargo said. "I think there's too much stacked against you." He became silent again, looked out the window, and saw that the night had stolen silently over the land. Thoughts raced through his head, pulling at him. They were taking on more than they knew, more than they had the men or experience to handle. And it was plain that Blakelock Haskell already knew of their plans. That was why he'd been so anxious to give his side of the picture, first. The entire scheme seemed one destined for failure, certainly for big trouble. He felt himself drawing back from it. Trouble came easy enough and often enough on its own. It was like cowshit. There was no need to deliberately step into it.

"What do you say, Fargo?" Barney McCall asked, cutting into his thoughts.

"I say go and try to make a better deal with Haskell," he told the man. "Now that he sees you're determined to make your own drive he might listen to reason."

"You know better, Fargo," Barney said. "He figures he holds all the cards no matter what we do."

Fargo grunted at the truth in the man's words. He felt for Barney McCall's plight, and the others' with him, but sympathy was one thing, stupidity another. "Will you lead us, Fargo?" he heard the man ask.

Fargo finished the whiskey, stood up. "I think you're biting off more than you can chew," he said. "I'll think on it, that's the most I can say now," he answered.

"I told you he wouldn't help us," Liz bit out, anger in her voice, and Fargo saw the green eyes grow dark.

"Now, Liz, easy does it," her uncle soothed. "The man said he'd think on it. That's enough for me."

"He's saying no the easy way," she snapped, glared at him.

Fargo nodded at Barney McCall and ignored the girl. "I'll stop by tomorrow and let you know," he said. "Good luck, no matter what."

He turned, walked from the house, aware of Liz Ryan's footsteps following him outside. She came up to him as he halted beside the pinto. "It seems Blanche Haskell did a good job last night," she slid at him.

41

He felt his brows lift. "Nighttime spying one of your talents?" he asked quietly.

"No spying," she snapped. "Just riding."

"At that hour?" he questioned.

"I like to ride at night before I turn in," she said.

"Instead of tossing and turning?" he said.

Her hand started up in an arc but she pulled it back. "Bastard," she muttered. "No, but then you wouldn't understand."

"Try me," he said.

"It's a private time, just me and the stars. It's a time to think, to feel, to be closer to things bigger than yourself," she answered, her chin lifted in defiance.

But she had touched a truth he knew and he understood and she'd said it about as well as it could be said unless you were a poet. "Not bad." He smiled.

She eyed him warily, belligerently. "You sound like you might understand." She sniffed.

"I just might." He laughed as he swung onto the pinto.

"But there's Blanche Haskell waiting," she snapped.

"That's right," he said amiably as her glare returned.

"And that's more important to your kind. It's a matter of having no conscience," she threw at him.

He smiled. "It's a matter of poking," he said mildly and watched her questioning frown appear. "I'd sure rather spend my time poking the front of a woman than the back of a steer," he finished, wheeled the pinto around, and cantered off, feeling her anger reaching after him.

"Bastard," she called out and he let the wind carry his laugh back. He disappeared into the darkness, crested the hill, and went down the other side, turned the pinto toward Blanche Haskell's house. It was still early and he let a thought take shape in his mind. Maybe he could still do Liz Ryan and the others a favor. Not exactly self-sacrifice, he admitted to himself, but doing a good deed didn't always need to be noble. You could enjoy two birds with one stone. He grinned and hurried the pinto on.

Blanche heard the sound of the horse, had the door open as he rode to a halt, her glance as much made of curiosity as surprise as he entered. He took a moment to enjoy the silk nightgown she wore, cut in a deep V in front, hardly holding in the deep, rounded breasts. As she moved, he glimpsed the brown-pink rounded edge of one of the wide areolas.

"Couldn't keep yourself away, I hope," Blanche said with laughter in the mist-gray eyes.

"Something like that," he answered. "I just came from seeing Liz Ryan and her uncle. Things aren't quite the way Cousin Blakelock put it last night."

"I imagine not," she said. "He's not above being careless with truth." Fargo nodded in admiration. She was fair enough. "Barney McCall give you their side of it?" she asked and Fargo nodded. "I'd guess he was just as careless with the truth," she added.

"Maybe," Fargo conceded. It was entirely possible, though somehow he didn't take Barney McCall as a lying man.

"Blakelock's just pressuring them to get his way," she said.

"I'm told there's been a damn sight more than pressuring," Fargo said. "I heard about murder and burning and night-riding terror."

"I've heard that, too, but it's pretty much all talk, their way of getting sympathy. There was good evidence the Olsons were killed by a passing pack of gunslingers," Blanche said.

"But what if it's the truth?" Fargo questioned.

"I can't answer for Blakelock or Fred," she said. "They may have gotten carried away with themselves or something just got out of hand. I say forget them, forget all of them."

"I'd like doing that but I'd feel better about it if your cousin would let up on the small ranchers. Let them alone. Let them do their thing. If they want to drive their herds south, let them. They'll have enough troubles."

"They asked you to help them," she said and he nodded, saw the mist-gray eyes studying him. "What are they to you? Why does it matter?" she questioned.

"Their strugglers, trying to make it. Maybe I'm a sucker for that. Or maybe I just think Cousin Blakelock's got more than enough for himself," Fargo said.

The gray eyes continued to study him. "You'd stay if I could get him to let up, to listen to me?" she asked.

"For a while," Fargo agreed.

Blanche looked away, frowning, into her own thoughts. "I don't know if he'd listen. He's stubborn," she said, returned her eyes to the Trailsman. "I can tell him you won't help them, that you'll stay here with me," she said.

"For a while," Fargo repeated.

"I'll talk to him. I'll do my best," she said, sliding arms around his neck. "And I'll make you change your mind about only staying for a while." He smiled inwardly. That had been tried before, often, always with the same results. But hell, she was entitled to try. He had no intention of stopping her. That'd be downright unfair to her. Her mouth found his, her tongue sliding out at once. No intention at all, he told himself as his hand slipped inside the nightgown, closed around one soft mound. She moaned, half-turned, pulled him with her as she led the way into the bedroom. He glimpsed the big double bed on a pine bedstand as she slid the filmy nightgown to the floor. He

44

had his gunbelt off as her hands joined his in unbuttoning, unsnapping, and in moments his flesh was against hers, soft, exciting touch, and she lay back on the bed as he pressed against her.

He ran his hand down her abdomen as she murmured. "I kept thinking about last night," she breathed. "All day. It was worse than not having at all." His hand moved over the mound of her belly, smooth convexity, through the black nap to hold at the warm wetness of her. "Go on, Jesus, go on," she cried out, reached down to press his fingers into her. He parted the wet, flaccid lips, fingers circling slowly, edging deeper until she was arching, trembling, crying out for him to go further in. "Don't tease me, don't, please," she protested as his fervor rose and he saw tiny beads of perspiration coat her forehead.

He felt her grow taut, lifted himself, swung over her, and slid smoothly into the waiting, wanting glove. Slowly, he moved back and forth, little movements as she cried out with each until with the abruptness he remembered from the night before, she arched upward and the scream rose, grew higher, still higher until it became a wailing sound, and she hung in the air, back arched, holding him with her. The scream held until suddenly she fell back, as a balloon drained of air collapses, lay with eyes closed, motionless, hardly breathing. He stayed with her, remembering again, till he finally moved to lie half-over her and watch the mist-gray eyes slowly come open, mistier and grayer than usual.

"Just as wonderful," she murmured.

"Why not?" he answered.

Her round shoulders gave a tiny shrug. "I was afraid it mightn't be," she said, rose to a sitting position, and he pulled himself up with her, took in the full-blown beauty of her breasts as they hung loosely.

"Tomorrow night?" she said.

He nodded. "Meanwhile, give me a good reason to turn away from Barney McCall's offer," he said.

"It'll work out. It's all been blown out of proportion. Don't believe what you've heard," she said as he pulled on clothes. She went to the door with him, a robe tossed around her voluptuousness, kissed him lingeringly. He listened to the soft click of the door as she closed it behind him. She'd do her best to reach Blakelock Haskell, he was certain. He rode slowly from the ranchhouse, let himself feel confident as well as satisfied. He cut across a field and through a brush-and-rock passage. He was relaxed, too relaxed, a little tired. He heard the sound just a fraction too late, his senses just a hair's breadth off. The shot exploded at almost the same instant, grazed his forehead, and he half-fell, half-dived from the pinto as the horse bolted forward. He'd just hit the ground when he felt the lariat go around him, thrown from one of the rocks above. He rolled but it tightened, pinning his arms to his side.

"Get him," he heard a voice say and saw the figures leaping down from both sides of the rocks, running from behind the scrub brush. He tried to get one hand to the Colt but the lariat was drawn tight and the figure rushed at him, yanking the gun out of the holster and flinging it aside. He saw a dirty yellow shirt, caught the blow coming in a swinging arc, and twisted away to take it alongside the temple. It nonetheless sent him sprawling to the ground, the lariat yanking hard against him. He lay there for a moment, looked up to see the figures in a semi-circle around him. The one holding the lariat had a big, bulbous nose that made a harsh face look clownlike. Two others were ordinary enough, one with a heavy leather jacket, the other wearing a silver spur as a pendant hanging from his neck. His eyes moved to the dirty

46

yellow shirt, the same one he had seen fall in behind Fred Haskell in town.

"You've made two mistakes, big boy," the yellow shirt snarled. "You didn't leave town when you were told to and you went visiting Barney McCall and that stuck-up niece of his."

"Tell Fred Haskell I do what I want to do," Fargo said as his eyes swept the four men.

The yellow-shirted one uttered a harsh laugh. "All we're going to tell Fred is that you're full of holes," he said.

Fargo felt the lariat pulled a notch tighter, the rope biting into the powerful muscles of his chest. His upper arms were immobilized against his sides by the rope but he could move from the elbows down. He let his right hand edge to the double-bladed Arkansas throwing knife that nestled in the leather holder strapped to his calf. His leg half under him as he lay on the ground, it seemed only that he was trying to push himself up straighter.

"Here?" he heard one of the men ask.

"No, somebody'll find him by morning," the dirty yellow shirt answered. "We'll do it by the river and toss him in." Fargo's hand touched the side of his calf, felt the outline of the knife in its sheath under his trouser leg. "Get him on his feet," the yellow shirt ordered.

Fargo watched the bulbous-nosed man holding the other end of the lariat start toward him, gathering in the rope as he neared. As the man began to pull up on the rope, momentarily blocking the other three from sight, Fargo's hand slipped under the edge of the trouser leg, closed around the slender handle of the double-edged, slim blade. The man, almost over him now, started to yank him up on his feet. In one lightning motion, Fargo whipped the blade out of the ankle sheath. Able to use only his lower arm, he arced the blade upward as the man bent half-over him, saw the razor-sharp steel rake the man's chest, tearing his shirt open, travel upward as far as his forearm would carry, embedding itself in the base of the man's throat. As Fargo raised his other arm to tear at the lariat, loosening it, a shower of red spurted from the man's throat first, then from the bulbous nose.

Fargo tore the lariat loose from himself as the man pitched forward, a rasping, death-rattle of a noise coming from him. "What the hell's goin' on?" he heard the yellow shirt growl. As the man pitched forward atop him, he yanked the bushwhacker's gun from its holster, pulling it out backward, spinning it around as he let the man's still-rasping form fall over him. He fired off three shots, not bothering to aim, saw the others dive away. One yanked his gun, fired, and Fargo felt the bullet slam into the body half atop him. He hit the ground, still holding the body as a shield, rolled, flung it aside, and dived into the brush as a fusillade of shots splayed around him. He rolled again, into deeper brush, halted, pulled up on one knee.

"Sonofabitch," he heard the yellow shirt shouting. "Jesus, he got Eddie." Another voice growled a reply, muffled, and Fargo peered through the brush but saw only the lifeless form of the man on the ground. He had fallen onto his back, the bulbous nose flowing claret to join the stream from the base of his throat. He looked like a clown whose makeup had somehow sneared.

"You bastard, you're as good as dead," he heard the yellow shirt shout, followed the direction of the voice. The man was to his right, in a cluster of oak scrub. Fargo stayed quiet as a stalking puma. "You hear me?" the man shouted again. He hadn't moved, Fargo noted. "You come out and maybe we'll let you high-tail out of here," the man said. A slow smile made of ice slipped over the Trailsman's face. All the talk was designed to keep his attention and, the smile still on his lips, he lowered himself almost to the ground. He let his eyes move to the left, to the brush at the other side. He'd only a few minutes to wait when he caught the tiny movement of leaves. "What do you say?" the yellow shirt called out.

Fargo's eyes held on the leaves as they moved again, saw the figure, shadowed shape, moving in a crouch through the brush to come up on him from the other side. "Let's talk," the yellow shirt shouted. "You got any cash? We'll make a deal." The man's voice was just so much noise to Fargo as his eyes stayed riveted on the shadowed figure. He raised the gun, glanced at it quickly, a Walker Colt. They always fired high and he dropped his sights a fraction, waited. The figure came into view again, closer now. The man paused to listen in his crouching progress. It was his final pause. Fargo's finger squeezed against the trigger and the gun erupted, bucked in his hand, but he saw the shot hit exactly where he'd aimed. The man's figure half-rose, seemed to gyrate and then topple out of the brush, the side of his face blown away.

"Goddamn," Fargo heard the voice snarl. He spun, not bothering with silence, darted deeper into the brush, then veered off, slid to a halt against the base of a line of rocks. Instantly, he was absolutely silent again, hardly breathing, half-sitting, half-leaning against an edge of rock. He could see across the clear space where they'd jumped him to the brush and rock on the other side. Two more to go, he murmured silently, his lips turned in grimly. They were being silent, too, now, scanning his side of the brush for anything that might be a target. All the talk had come to an end. Without so much as disturbing the air, Fargo reached out, gathered a handful of pebbles in his fingers. He tossed them to the left where they clattered against the rock with the sound of someone slipping down the stone. The two shots flashed in the darkness, one almost opposite, the other further to the left. The bullets pinged against the rocks and Fargo focused on where the gunfire flashes had come.

He drew a sight on the one to the left, squinted into the night. Raising the Walker Colt again, he rested his right arm against the rock, gathered another handful of pebbles in his left hand. He tossed half to his right, the other half to his left as he kept his eyes trained on the spot across from him. The two gunshots flashed as the small stones landed, following the sound, firing first at one spot, then at the other. Fargo, his gun already steadied, raised and waiting, the sight trained on the area, fired one shot a split-second after the second flash. He heard the gutteral cry of pain, cut off in the middle, a low wheezed gasp and the sound of a body falling into the brush. The moment he fired, he dived down to flatten himself and felt the two bullets as they hurtled over his head and into the rock where he'd been leaning.

He lay flat, his lips drawn back. Only one left, the dirty yellow shirt. He wanted answers from the man, confirmations, really. He holstered the Walker Colt, silently moved from his prone position, lifting himself up with his palms pressed flat on the ground, listened. Only silence greeted him. His foe knew it had come down to the final line. The man had retreated into his own silent waiting, watching for him to make a slip, one error that could spell death. He had obviously decided that was his best chance and, indeed it was, Fargo knew, matching silence with silence, playing the waiting game. The icy smile touched Fargo's lips again. He'd not be drawn into the man's decision. Never play your opponent's game. It was a rule he always followed. No matching silences. He'd bring the man into the open, make him make a move.

The icy smile stayed with him as Fargo moved to his right, making short, abrupt spurts of motion yet staying hidden. He made no effort at silence now. In halting, erratic fashion, he began to circle toward the pinto and the other horses, still darting in short spurts, halting, darting forward again. The man could trace his progress by the sound of it, Fargo knew, and he saw that his foe continued to remain silent, refusing to risk more hurried shots. Fargo circled in the thick brush, began to near the place where the pinto waited. Halting, he heard the sudden sound of movement in the brush across the open stretch of land and he half-laughed. The man had suddenly realized his goal.

Fargo darted forward again, another flurried movement that brought him closer to the pinto. He whistled softly, saw the horse's ears prick up. The sleek black-and-white form turned toward him, started to move to the edge of the brush. The man watched, Fargo knew, growing nervous as the pinto now blocked his view. He'd have his gun aimed, ready to blast off shots. The pinto moved closer, stepped forward again, and Fargo watched with narrowed eyes. His move had to be perfectly timed. Split-seconds would count and there'd be no room for miscalculation. The pinto was no more than two feet from him now. He rose on the balls of his feet, felt the powerful muscles of his calves grow taut, pressed down, and sprang, catapulting himself upward through the brush. He hit the pinto's saddle, got one hand on the horn, and pulled himself up, flattening down across the horse's withers, all in one motion. Three shots blasted into the night as the pinto bolted forward, two hurtling inches over his flattened form, the third going through the shoulder of his jacket.

He stayed glued down across the pinto's neck and heard the man's curse of fury, the sound of racing footsteps and, moments later, the hoofbeats of his horse taking up the chase. It had worked. He'd been drawn into the open and Fargo rose up in the saddle, sent the pinto down a passage between the rocky brush. Another passage appeared, bordered by jutting slabs of rock on both sides. He heard his pursuer riding hard to catch up to him and he reined the horse to a halt, waited. The other horse came to a halt at once and Fargo's eyes were ice blue. The man was taking no chances. He was playing it carefully and Fargo sent the pinto galloping forward again, heard the other horse break into pursuit at once. He turned to follow the path as it curved, saw a ledge of rock shoulder high, slowed the pinto almost to a halt as it came abreast of it. Reaching out with both hands, he grasped hold of the thin edge, pulled himself up out of the saddle, and swung onto the ledge. He reached down, slapped the pinto on the rump, and the horse bolted forward. Fargo pressed himself flat on the ledge and waited.

He had but a few moments to wait as he spied the dirty yellow shirt come into view, the man riding hard, chasing the sound of the pinto. As he came to the ledge, Fargo dove forward, hitting his target squarely. He went down over the other side of the horse, twisting to land on his feet while the man, taken by surprise, landed hard on his side, and Fargo heard his grunt of pain. He was trying to roll over as Fargo yanked him around by his dirty yellow shirt, smashed a short, arcing blow to the man's face. The man flew backward to hit the ground. "I know Fred Haskell sent you but I want to hear you say it," he growled.

The man's hand dropped down to his gun but Fargo's foot kicked out with the speed of a rattler's strike, caught the man's wrist. "Ow, Jesus!" the man cried out in pain, his hand falling away. Fargo reached down, yanked the gun from the holster, and flung it aside. He reached down with both hands, yanked the man to his feet.

"Rotten, bushwhacking bastard," he snarled. "Let's hear it."

The man tried an underhand, sweeping blow to the groin and Fargo half-twisted, managed to take the blow on the side of his thigh. He let go of the yellow shirt and slammed a downward right to the man's face, saw it crack the skin and a rush of red stream down the man's cheek. Fargo followed with a quick left that landed on the man's cheekbone and he saw the red welt begin immediately. The man lowered his head, tried to rush the big, black-haired man. As he roared forward, Fargo brought up a short right, felt it rip the man's upper lip and tear into a part of his nose. He danced to the side, brought a whistling left around and felt it smash into the side of the man's face. The dirty yellow shirt dropped down as the man fell onto one knee, his face bleeding from at least four places, his cheekbone puffed out of shape. Fargo slammed a straight right into the face, saw the man hurtle backward to hit the ground stretched out completely.

He stepped forward, reached down, and pulled the figure up by the dirty yellow shirt, felt the garment rip in two, grabbed one of the torn pieces, and yanked again. The man's torso came up, his face looking like a badly bruised slab of butcher's meat. He shook the man, saw his eyes slowly come into focus. "You going to answer me or do I break you in little pieces?" he rasped. He raised his fist again, saw the fear come into the man's eyes.

"Yeah, Fred," the man choked out. "He told us."

Fargo's fist stayed poised. "The way he had you do other killings and burnings," Fargo said and the man nodded. Fargo flung him away and he sprawled on the ground. "I ought to make you found in a grave but

I want you to go back to your boss," he said. "I want him to know I know." He stepped forward, yanked the man up by his arm, sent him stumbling toward his horse. "Get on and high-tail it out of here before I change my mind," he growled. The man turned, wiping some of the blood from his face on his torn shirt, painfully climbed into the saddle. Fargo watched him ride slowly down the passageway to disappear into the darkness.

He picked up the Walker Colt, pushed it into his holster, and whistled sharply. The pinto appeared a few moments later and came to him. Fargo stroked the horse's shiny black head and swung into the saddle. He drew a deep breath and began to ride back, retracing steps. He wanted to return to where they'd first bushwhacked him and retrieve his own gun. The heavy Walker Colt was a poor substitute for his own Colt .45. He rode back slowly, his eyes narrowed in thought, anger simmering inside him, and he'd almost reached the place where he'd been attacked when he reined to a halt, still inside the rock-lined passageway.

The sense of danger had come to him suddenly, the way it always did. Sixth sense, intuition, a gut feeling, the instinct born of his one-quarter Cherokee heritage, whatever it was, he'd had it before and it had never failed him. Tiny stirrings inside him, the prickling at the back of his neck, a sudden stab of coldness that shuddered through the body, the same instinctive knowing that lets a wild creature sense danger before it sees, hears, or smells it. Whatever made it happen, it was a sometime thing that didn't always make itself known. The veneer of civilized man got in the way too often, but when it did he had learned to pay heed.

His eyes strained to peer ahead but he saw nothing. Yet danger lay near and he slipped from the saddle, paused for a moment with his eyes cold as a winter lake. The man would have ridden back this way, too, and Fargo's lips grew thin. He turned, found a good-sized clump of scrub brush, and pulled it out of the ground in one piece. It came reluctantly, roots clinging to the soil. He lifted it, saw that it was bulky enough for his purpose, and placed it atop the saddle. Running a length of lariat through it and under the pinto's belly, he tied it in place, then removed his jacket and draped it over the brush, put his hat on top of it. The brush made enough bulk so that in the darkness, with his jacket and hat over, it looked like his upper torso sitting slightly slumped in the saddle.

He touched the pinto lightly on the rump and the horse moved forward. Fargo followed, moving in a crouching lope, staying back a half-doezn yards. The pinto neared the place of the original ambush, started down the incline of the passageway to the wider area, and Fargo stayed behind, the Walker Colt in his hand. The pinto had just emerged from the passageway when the shots rang out, two, both slamming into the jacketed shape on the saddle. Fargo saw the dirty yellow shirt, the man standing on a flat rock to the right, the rifle still at his shoulder. He was just starting to lower the gun when Fargo fired, steadying himself on one knee, a single shot from the Walker Colt, aimed a fraction low. The figure half-twisted, slowly, as if it were held by an unseen string. The rifle fell from the man's hands to land with a sharp clatter against the rock and the torn yellow shirt flapped in the wind as the man toppled forward, almost as though he were diving. He hit the base of the rock and Fargo heard his neck snap but the man was already dead, he knew.

Fargo rose, walked forward, stared down at the man as he lay with his neck crumpled into his shoulders, the rifle nearby. He lifted his gaze, saw the empty rifle holster beside the saddle of one of the other horses. The man had returned to the spot planning to try again for a final ambush. "Stupid bastard,"

Fargo muttered aloud as he dropped the Walker Colt on the lifeless form. He turned away, searched for a moment until he found his own gun where they had thrown it, pushed it into the holster. He dismantled the crude dummy, donned his jacket and hat, and rode from the spot. It'd take a little longer for Fred Haskell to find out what had happened but he'd know soon enough, Fargo thought as he rode. He had headed the pinto toward Rawley, suddenly changed direction and cantered over a ridge and down the other side, kept on until he pulled to a halt in front of Blanche Haskell's ranchhouse. She took a few moments to answer his pounding on the door, stared at him, a robe drawn around her nightdress. He saw her take in the dirt smudges on his face, the hard coldness of his eyes as she opened the door further for him to step inside.

"I've a message for you to take back," he growled.

She continued to frown up at him. "What happened?" she asked.

"Four of Fred Haskell's bushwhackers just tried to blow me away," the Trailsman said, his voice made of ice.

The surprise in her face was real. "Oh, my God. Oh, Fargo, I'm sorry," she said.

"He's going to be sorrier," Fargo clipped out. "And it's true, all the rest, the killing and the terror. It's all come out of the same place."

Blanche Haskell turned away for a moment, her face tight. "Blakelock has a stupid son. I've told him that before. I'll tell him again," she said.

"Yes, he's stupid but his pa is smart. He just looks the other way when it suits him to do so. It lets him play innocent but they're a tandem hitch, one behind the other," Fargo said.

Her mist-gray eyes held his angry stare. "I don't

know," she murmured. "I don't know what to think or what to say."

"I'll tell you what to say. Tell Blakelock Haskell I'm taking the offer the small ranchers gave me," he told her.

Her face clouded and she pressed hands against his chest. "Don't do it, Fargo. You said yourself you didn't want to get involved."

"I got involved. Fred Haskell involved me," Fargo snapped.

"You don't have to strike back. Maybe he'll learn from this. I'll talk to Blakelock," she tried.

"That won't help any. This kind of thing's been a part of their operation all along. That's damn plain now," Fargo returned.

"Stay here with me. Help me convince Blakelock to stop it," she said. "Stay here, Fargo. You agreed you would if I could get Blakelock to cooperate."

"I said maybe but that maybe was shot down tonight," he answered. "And he won't back off. I know that, now."

She leaned her forehead against his chest, her voice low, murmuring. "It's not fair to blame me for tonight, to take it out on me," she said.

He lifted her face up gently. "I'm not blaming you. Maybe there'll be another time for staying, after your relatives learn it's everybody's world and not just theirs." He pulled back, opened the door, paused another moment. "Tell Cousin Blakelock that if he's smart he'll back off," Fargo warned.

She nodded solemnly. "I'll tell him, I promise," she said and he left her, rode back to Rawley, got there a little before the dawn, and stabled the pinto. In his little room at the hotel, he undressed and lay naked across the bed until sleep finally pushed aside his anger.

4

It was midmorning when he woke and swung from the bed. The events of the night stayed with him, like a sour taste in the mouth. When he finished washing in water too cold for comfort, he dressed and fetched the pinto from the stable, gave the horse a quick brushing, and saddled him. He mounted, moved slowly down the street, halted where a tall man with a thin beard faced a semicircle of at least a dozen others. He recognized the man at once. He had seen him at Blakelock Haskell's ranch during his visit.

"But we heard you were hiring range hands," one of the semicircle of men said. "This some kind of rotten joke?"

"No, you heard right," Haskell's hand said. "But not this morning, maybe not today."

"That's what you told us yesterday," another of the men said. "What're you waitin' for?"

"Word from the boss. It'll come soon as he's sure how many he can take on," Haskell's man answered. Fargo moved on as the other grumbled, his lake-blue eyes narrowing for a moment. He rode on a dozen yards, drew abreast of the bank, and reined up as he saw the Basket Phaeton there, its delicate lines so contrasting to the drays and rack wagons nearby. He sidled over to it as Blanche stepped from the bank. She wore a gray outfit that matched her gray eyes and saw him at once as she climbed into the carriage. Her face sober, almost petulant, turned to him as he halted alongside her.

"Talked to him yet?" he asked casually.

"Just came from there," she said. "Fred went looking for his four hands and found them. He wasn't happy. I had a few strong things to say, also. Altogether a very nasty scene." She peered at Fargo, saw his face masked, expressionless. "Last night was all Fred's idea, Blakelock told me," she said.

"Was it, now?" Fargo grunted derisively. "Fred Haskell does what he does because he knows he can get away with it. They're a tandem hitch, I told you."

She half-shrugged, looked unhappy. "Blakelock was genuinely upset," she said.

"Sure he was. It turned out bad," Fargo said. "He's out four hands and I learned about all his smooth talk being so much steer shit."

A slight-built man hurried from the bank to interrupt her answer, waving a small piece of paper in one hand. "Miss Haskell, you forgot your deposit slip," he said.

"Thank you, Mr. Simons," Blanche said, taking the slip.

"Can't have a five-thousand-dollar deposit slip for your special account lying around, can we?" The man smiled gratuitously.

"No, we can't," Blanche said with a trace of annoyance in her voice, tucked the deposit slip into a small bag at her side. She gave the man a glance of dismissal and he half-smiled, hurried back into the bank.

"Five thousand," Fargo echoed slowly. "You can buy a lot of seeds to cross-breed with that kind of money."

"Yes, but it has to last for the year," she said. Her hand reached out to touch his arm. "There's more to tell but not here. Let's talk again, please? Come back with me now?"

"Later," he said. "I'll stop by later."

She nodded, turned from him, her face grave,

snapped the reins, and the carriage moved away. He watched her drive off, her back very straight, and he felt a rush of sympathy for her. Bad relatives were always a problem. He turned, rode from town, made his way over the low hills directly to Barney McCall's small ranch, eased past the herd rubbing against the corral fences. The man came from the house to greet him as he swung down from the saddle. Liz Ryan followed, her slender figure clothed in Levi's and a heavy checked cotton work shirt. But the smallish breasts still managed to push themselves out saucily. She halted back a few paces, the brown-flecked eyes now dark green.

"Where do you figure to drive your herds to in New Mexico?" he asked Barney McCall.

"Socorra. That's south of Albuquerque," the man said.

"And across the Rio Grande," Fargo grunted. His eyes grew hard as he thought aloud. "A long drive. Long, hard, and dangerous. There's no saying I can get your herds there, no promises except trouble."

He let the words sink in, watched the man's face slowly come to realization, break into a wide grin. "No, no promises. Hot damn, you hear that, Liz? The Trailsman going to take us. *Hot Damn!*" Barney McCall shouted.

"One thing," Fargo said sternly. "I call all the shots. No arguments, no matter what I decide. Everybody agrees to that."

"Oh, they'll agree, you just know that," the man said, starting to hurry to a brown quarterhorse nearby. "I'll go tell them right now," he said.

"You said you could put enough hands together. I want them here, all of them. I want to check them out for myself," Fargo said as the man pulled himself into the saddle.

"This afternoon," Barney McCall said. "I'll have them all here this afternoon, everybody that's going."

"I'll be back then," Fargo said and the man raced off at once. Fargo's eyes met the girl's as she stepped forward, saw her studying, appraising stare.

"Why?" she asked. "Why'd you decide to help us?"

There were thorns in her voice and he allowed her a slow smile. "Sometimes I like to buck the odds," he offered. Her eyes continued to hold back acceptance. "Or maybe I figure to collect all I won in the race," he added.

Her eyes found green fire. "Then you can figure again," she snapped.

His frown was injured. "You made a bet to the winner. Gambling debts are debts of honor. You telling me you've no honor?" he asked.

"I've a damn sight more than you, I'll wager," she tossed back.

"There you go betting again." He grinned.

Liz Ryan's lips tightened and she lifted her chin and the sunlight made her handsome face a thing of light and dark planes. "Why'd you decide to help us?" she asked again doggedly.

"My reasons," he snapped back curtly. "I'm doing it, that's all you have to know."

He started to turn away, one hand on the saddle horn. "Blanche Haskell say no to you?" he heard her slide out waspishly.

His smile was broad as he met her eyes. "You'd like thinking that, wouldn't you?" he said. "But you know better."

She pressed her lips onto each other, her face suddenly taking on an angry half-pout. "I'd like to hear the real reason," she muttered.

"Maybe someday, if and when I feel like it," he said and climbed onto the pinto. He rode away after another quick grin at her. She was a defiant, fiery little piece, full of the pride of the underdog. He laughed to himself as he rode back across the hills. He'd almost swung onto the dirt road leading to Blanche Haskell's place when he saw the riders moving along the road, over a dozen of them. Haskell's man with the thin beard led them and he watched them go on in the direction of the Haskell ranch. Blakelock Haskell had obviously come through with the order to hire. Fargo rode on, wondering idly what had held up the man's hiring and prompted his sudden go ahead. Perhaps Haskell had waited to see which way the cards were falling, Fargo speculated. The answer was reasonable and he wondered why it didn't satisfy. Range hands or gunslingers, he grunted inwardly. He'd learn soon enough.

Blanche Haskell's place came into view and he saw the three men in the long fields of green crops, weeding and hoeing. Blanche was at the door as he dismounted, her face searching his as she drew him inside. Her arms were around him at once. "I'm afraid, Fargo," she murmured. "Blakelock's angry. It's not even sure that he can hold Fred in line."

Fargo pulled back from her, didn't hide the cynicism in his voice. "He can, if he's a mind to," he answered.

"There'll be trouble. Blakelock won't just sit by and let them make their drive, Fargo," she said. "He's too convinced he's right."

"I figured as much," Fargo said.

"Tell them to hold off on their drive," Blanche said.

"That's not my decision," he said.

Her face was despairing. "If you don't lead them they'll wait. They'd listen to you. Give me more time to work on Blakelock. Just give me more time to get through to him."

"And if you don't?" Fargo asked. "I can't hold

things back. He or that rotten son of his might decide to see that the small ranchers never get their drive going. I can't take that chance."

Her gray eyes grew a shade darker as she peered at him. "I don't want to see anything happen to you," she said. "Why do you insist on sticking your life on the line for them? If you help them this time they'll still be small grubbers struggling to keep their heads above water. Don't you see that? They're really not worth it."

"You're sounding like your Cousin Blakelock," Fargo commented.

"I'm trying to reach you, dammit," she exploded. "I care about you. I want you here with me."

He touched her cheek with the back of his hand. "Sorry, I'm grateful to you for that. But you're chasing the wrong thought on this," he told her.

"Why?"

"It's not whether they're worth it. Most likely some are and some aren't but that's no matter. It's what they stand for that counts. Sure, most of them will still be grubbers afterward. The point is they've a right to be grubbers, to struggle and keep trying. They've a right to be little and that's the heart of it."

Her face held anger. "You're talking principles and I'm talking people."

"They go together, principles and people, like ham and eggs, whether we like it or not," he returned.

The mist-gray eyes held steady. "You going to lead them down the usual route to Abilene? Blakelock knows that like the back of his hand. He'll be waiting for you," she said.

"No, I'm not even driving down to Abilene," Fargo said. "I won't play his game. He'll have to come after me."

"Not to Abilene?" She frowned. "Where?"

"West, first," he said. "The less you know the better for you."

"Yes, of course," Blanche agreed, her arms sliding around his chest. "Promise me one thing. If it goes real bad, pack it in. Come back. I'll be waiting. Don't be a fool over this."

"Never." He grinned, kissed her quickly. "I'm not the martyr type." He stepped back, pulled the door open, and left, not glancing back as he climbed onto the pinto and rode off. He'd almost stayed but that would have only made it worse for her. She was torn apart enough now, seeing Blakelock Haskell for the first time, perhaps, yet unable to stop excusing him. Seeing comes hard sometimes, especially when blood relations are involved. But she'd find her way through. Blanche Haskell moved from a deep streak of contained independence, he grunted to himself and rode on. He halted at a small stream and let the pinto drink of the cool, clear water, then took the time to wash the trail dust from the horse until the coat was its usual gleaming white and shining black. When the afternoon grew long, he rode on to Barney McCall's place.

The others were there, waiting, he saw as he neared, horses and buckboards gathered to one side, a small group standing outside the house. Fargo rode up, swung down from the pinto, and Barney McCall stepped forward, a wide smile on his face. "Got everybody here for you." The man beamed. Fargo's eyes moved over those gathered in front of him. *I don't believe this*, he heard himself say silently. *I don't believe what I'm seeing.* He turned to Barney McCall, stared at the man.

"Are you for real?" he asked. "Are these your rangehands for the drive or are you making some kind of joke?"

"Now, I know they don't seem like what you had

in mind," the man said placatingly. "I know they're not what you expected."

Fargo continued to stare at the man incredulously. "You can sure as hell say that again," he growled. His eyes flicked up to where Liz Ryan watched and he shook his head in disbelief. Slowly, he let his glance travel over the group again. "Damn, I don't believe it," he repeated, aloud this time.

Barney McCall interrupted. "I know what you're thinking," he began and Fargo cut him off.

"Hell you do and I don't want to say it out loud," he snapped.

"Just meet these good folks, Fargo," Barney McCall pleaded. "Just meet them." Fargo stared at him again, his frown drawing down his black, thick brows as Barney McCall touched his arm, edged him toward the others. "This here is Henrietta Baker, Fargo," the man introduced.

Fargo stared at the woman, disbelief inside him becoming a kind of incredulous anger. He guessed her to be sixty-five, maybe seventy years of age, white-haired, a tight-skinned, somewhat hawklike face, a high-necked black dress on a form narrow and straight as a ramrod.

"Don't look at me that way, young feller," Henrietta Baker snapped out, her face growing more hawklike. "I was herding and roping steers while you were still in knee pants. So don't be looking down your nose at me."

Sharp-tongued old biddy, Fargo murmured inwardly. The kind used to giving orders. "No, ma'm," he said. "I just don't figure a cattle drive is a place for antiques."

He saw her jaw drop as he turned from her to take in the next figure, a man wearing a minister's collar and a minister's benevolent smile on his round face. Two flaxen-haired girls flanked him, early teens Fargo guessed, and identical twins, absolute copies of one another. Fargo stared at them and decided there was no way of telling them apart. Both had blossoming young bodies, both in Levi's and white cotton blouses, both with the same round, high breasts that thrust forward, and both the identical expressions, bold sultriness only half-covered by smiles.

"Reverend Richards and the twins, Carrie and Cassie," Barney McCall introduced. "Carrie and Cassie do all the herding on the Reverend's spread. They're very good."

"Hallelujah," Fargo bit out, looked from one girl to the other. It was like seeing double. They stood as one, hands on hips, their blue eyes assessing him with a frank boldness. "How old are you?" he growled.

"Sixteen," they answered together.

"Wonderful," Fargo almost spat.

"I prayed for the help we needed and the Lord sent you to us," the Reverend intoned.

"He's got a lousy sense of humor," Fargo muttered.

Barney turned him to the next couple, a young boy beside them, twelve or thirteen years old, Fargo guessed. "Bart and Sandra Dodd," Barney introduced. The man nodded out of an unsmiling, lined face that couldn't look anything but dour. He was at least twenty-five years older than the woman, Fargo estimated, met her brown eyes. Sandra Dodd had a rounded face, a little too fleshy but not unattractive, a good full figure with a narrow waist beneath billowy breasts. She met his eyes and he saw the signs of a woman grown restless in a dull, empty marriage, perhaps originally of convenience. He smiled inwardly. The signs were always there, never obvious, a glance, a stance, lips and hips, a subtle air most people couldn't pick up. He wasn't one of them. "Bobby's only twelve but he's a real good range rider," Fargo heard Barney McCall say and the man nodded toward the boy. Fargo's glance at the man didn't need words.

He turned to the next one, found himself before a big woman, six feet in height, shoulders like a cow moose, a flat face with black hair cut short, sharp brown eyes, and sensuous lips that seemed out of place. Large breasts swayed loosely under a smock dress. "Howdy," she said in a low voice.

"Amanda Koster," Barney introduced. The woman put one hand on the shoulder of a blond young woman beside her, hair worn in two long braids, a cheerful face and creamy breasts that pushed up from the square-cut neckline of a peasant blouse.

"This is Sophie," the woman said. Sophie smiled brightly out of a pink-cheeked face. She was really quite a big girl, Fargo realized, and looked smaller only because she was standing next to Amanda Koster.

"Amanda runs her ranch all by herself except for a handyman and Sophie," Barney McCall said. "Sophie came from Germany five years ago."

"Great," Fargo muttered. A woman with three young sons was next.

"Mrs. Downer and Jeff, Jim, and Jack," Barney said. "The boys are all expert cowhands." Fargo nodded, took in the young, eager faces, turned to the next in line, two men and a woman, all three sturdy of build with faces made of hard work. "The Sturdivents, Bess, Harry, and brother Sam," Barney McCall said. Fargo nodded again, went to the next, the last three in line, young men, lean, hard, trim figures. "Ed Norbert, Tom Sewall, Billy Walsh," Barney introduced. "They've made a ranch out of land nobody said could be used. Good men, Fargo."

Fargo agreed with a glance. They were three who could pull their weight, but as he turned away, his eyes sweeping back over the others, the anger spiraled inside him again.

"Twenty-one, counting Liz and myself," Barney McCall said and there was pride in his voice.

Fargo found himself staring in disbelief at the man. "Twenty-one," he repeated. "Women, girls, youngsters, a minister, an old lady, a twelve-year old, and maybe four or five good men. These are your range-hands?" The man shrugged. "You're out of your mind, all of you," Fargo added.

He saw Liz Ryan had stepped forward, green eyes on him. "We'll make it," she said. "I know we can."

"Sure you do, just the way you were sure of winning that race," he tossed back at her, saw her face harden in anger.

"That was a low blow," she returned.

"And this is a joke," Fargo said coldly.

"These folks can do a lot more than you think they can, Fargo," Barney McCall put in.

Cassie and Carrie stepped forward before he could answer, their eyes edging haughtiness, blond hair tossing, both pairs of high breasts standing out sharply beneath the white blouses.

"We can ride," the one said.

"We can rope," the other added.

"We can do anything," the first one said.

"And everything," the other finished. "Watch."

Jesus, they even talked in pairs, Fargo grunted silently as they spun, ran to two gray geldings, bounced onto the horses in unison. Blond hair streaming out behind them, they broke into a gallop, sent the two grays into a tight circle, weaved and cut in and cut out again, all but brushing each other. They stood in the stirrups, then the saddles, came down to do a belly turn under the racing horses and swing up into the saddle again, yelling with joy at every turn. They halted as abruptly as they'd started, leaped down from the horses to stand in front of Fargo, both wearing wide smiles, their eyes laughing.

"On a cattle drive you ride hard not fancy," he said coldly, saw their faces fall. His glance went beyond them to the others. "Any drive is hard, full of the unexpected. It takes stamina, strength, and most of all, experienced hands who know the strains of a drive. This one will take more of everything. You need the best hands you can get, not the worst."

"We figure we have the best trailsman," McCall said softly. "You said you'd help us."

"I did and you said you'd a crew of experienced rangehands," Fargo threw back and saw the man look uncomfortable.

"We can do it," Billy Walsh called out. "Hell, we've got to. We've no other choice."

"The Lord is with us," the minister added.

Fargo's eyes surveyed the group. The twins saw it as an exciting lark, maybe a chance to break loose. The Downer boys saw it as an adventure, the Reverend as a crusade. Henrietta Baker saw it as a last fling at playing young again. Only a few saw it realistically and they couldn't let themselves admit it. Liz Ryan was one, he was certain, behind those green eyes a down-to-earth realism.

"I've pledged my three boys to it," Mrs. Downer said quietly. "We've pledged our lives."

Fargo's lips pursed at words more true than she realized. Lives had been pledged and many would be forfeited. "We can do it with your help," he heard Reverend Richards call out.

"Well, Fargo, what do you say?" Barney McCall asked.

Fargo shrugged, drew a deep sigh from the soles of his boots. He'd take them as far as the dream would go. Not very far if Fred and Blakelock Haskell had their way. But he'd made a promise and they'd taken new heart from it, that was plain enough. They deserved at least one try at it.

"I'll stand by what I said," Fargo told them. "Maybe Haskell's boys will laugh themselves to death."

He heard the small shout of joy rise, swept away by a gust of wind, perhaps no faster than reality would sweep away their dreams. "Bless you," Reverend Richards called out. "The Lord will reward you, my boy."

"He'd better," Fargo growled.

The others began to move toward their wagons and horses. "I'll start here in the morning and pick up the rest of your herds along the way," he told them.

"We'll be ready," Ed Norbert said.

"One more thing," Fargo called out. "I'm sure you've all got a couple dozen steers you don't figure to take, old-timers, past market prime."

"Sure thing," Tom Sewall answered for everyone.

"Bring them," Fargo said.

"Bring them?" Sewall frowned. "What in hell for?"

"Just bring them. I'll think of something," Fargo said. "I call the shots, remember. No questions, no arguments."

"Yes, sir," the man answered. The twins paused and Fargo met their eyes, little hints of something circling inside their identical orbs.

"We do a lot of things. You'll see," one said.

He let one brow lift. They were probing, tossing out cryptic messages. "How do I tell you apart?" he asked.

"Easy. I'm Cassie," the one answered.

"And I'm Carrie," the other said. They broke out in gales of giggly laughter as they rode off. Identical rear ends, too, Fargo noted, moving in exactly the same way. They possessed a sassy sexiness and little wheels were definitely going around in their collective heads. He'd find out soon enough, he was certain. He watched Sandra Dodd drive the buckboard, her husband seated next to her, hands folded, Bobby in the rear. He saw her eyes lingering on him as she drove past. She turned off the interest in them when she caught his glance on her. He started to turn, saw Liz Ryan coming toward him, the green eyes cool. Her nice, square shoulders were thrust back and they made the upturned, smallish breasts poke tiny, sharp dots in the checked shirt.

"You don't think it can succeed, do you?" she said. "You don't believe in them."

"I don't have to believe," he said, saw her eyebrows lift. "Believing's for the Reverend."

"What's for you?" she asked.

"I just have to try," he said.

She considered the answer thoughtfully. "I guess that's all we can ask," she said.

"You guess right," he commented.

"Why do you want the extra stock? You've a reason," she said.

"Maybe." He smiled.

"Dammit, Fargo, I think some answers are in order," she flared.

"When I'm ready," he said. "I'll see you in the morning."

"You could stay the night here. There's room," she said.

"I'll be here come morning," he said, swung onto the pinto.

"A last night with Blanche Haskell?" he heard her toss out.

His smile was affable. "Wrong again. That makes twice," he said.

She furrowed her brow. "Twice?"

"Yep. She has a good figure," he said as he rode off and felt the hiss of anger following him. He returned to town and it was dark by the time he stabled the pinto. He went to the hotel room carrying a small parchment folder from his saddle bag. In the quiet of the room, he undressed to his trousers, opened the parchment folder, and spread it out across the narrow bed. It was not a map, not in the real sense of the word, but a guide, hand-drawn, a good part by himself. It traced passages, held names, guideposts, markings, not so much for accuracy but signposts reminders, spurs for the memory.

He lay down across the bed, studied the markings, closed his eyes, and let memories fill in details and supply the missing pieces. Finally he folded the parchment away, took off his trousers, and slept. The morning would come too soon, a morning when he'd feel more like a jester leading a pack of clowns than the Trailsman.

5

Liz was just herding the last of the steers from the corral as he rode up. She wore a light-green shirt and the morning sun slanted off the high planes of her face and she looked especially handsome. He watched her as she shepherded the steers together, leaning from one side of the saddle to the other, the movement causing first one, then the other upturned breast to press tight against the shirt. Barney, sitting atop a chuck wagon, waved to him. "I've drawn the job of cook," the man called out. "You go on with Liz. I'll be coming up behind."

Fargo waved back, helped round up a half-dozen straying steers, and settled in at the back of the herd, letting Liz lead. By midmorning they had collected everyone else and the herd, now grown considerably, moved slowly with a loose unity. He watched the three Downer boys ride the right edge of the herd, Ed Norbert and Tom Sewall staying in close at the left. A long black dress and white hair glinted atop a sturdy quarterhorse and Fargo watched Henrietta Baker ride down a straying steer, turn it smoothly, and bring it back into the herd without disturbing any of the others.

"How's that, sonny?" she called out as she rode by with a triumphant glare and Fargo gave her a nod of approval. She was a hard-fighting old gal, he had to admit with an inward smile. Another time and another place he could be admiring of her. Here he still wished for a lean, hard cowpoke forty years her junior. He spurred the pinto to the front of the herd, swung in beside Tom Sewall, the twins a few yards away, their eyes on him.

"Head them due west," he told the man. "Swing 'em around. We're making for Colorado Territory."

He rode to the right as the man began to push the lead steers in a slow turn and he watched Cassie and Carrie pitch in expertly. The three Downer boys came up to lend a hand in turning the huge, unwieldy mass of livestock. Fargo scooted a few uncooperative yearlings back into place and by noon the herd was moving west.

"How was that, Mister Trailsman?" one of the twins asked smugly as she rode up alongside him, the other one coming in beside her. He caught the faint laughter, smug and self-satisfied, in the question.

"Not bad," he admitted. He met their eyes as they moved up and down his hard-muscled frame with bold directness.

"You married?" one asked, eyes full of mischief.

"No," he said. "Cassie?" he guessed.

"Carrie." She laughed.

"Why not?" the other one asked.

"Having too much fun," he answered blandly.

"I'll bet," they chorused. "Fun, like lusting after women?" Carrie tossed out, laughing.

"Wherever and whenever," he said and saw the quick glance exchanged between them.

"Daddy would say that a man who lusteth after women is a sinner," Cassie said.

"And I say one who doesn't is either dead or a damn fool," Fargo answered. They rode off with squeals and giggles, high, outthrust breasts bounding in unison. Fargo's glance roamed back over the herd, watched Bobby Dodd riding herd along with Ed Norbert. The twelve-year-old was good, he saw, shifted his eyes to the wagons that rolled along beside the herd, four besides Barney McCall's chuck wagon. Sandra Dodd drove one, a canvas-covered, big California rack bed with heavy mountain-wagon brakes and a leaf-spring driver's seat. Her husband rode alongside on a thin brown horse. The Reverend drove the second wagon, a pared-down Conestoga. The German girl, Sophie, blond braids tossing, drove a seed-bed wagon with high sides and a homemade tarpaulin covering, as Amanda Koster rode herd nearby. Mrs. Downer drove the fourth wagon, a converted farm wagon with a canvas cover.

He moved around the herd, passed Liz Ryan, and saw her watch him curiously as he rode on, up a low hill and across the top line of it. He halted, his eyes sweeping the terrain, probing for signs foreign to the land. There was nothing, but then he didn't expect trouble yet and he rode back to the herd. He called a halt for rest a little past noon and his rangehands took turns gathering at the chuck wagon for coffee. He wandered over as Bart Dodd emptied his tin cup, Sandra standing nearby, a dark blue cotton dress holding her billowy breasts in tightly but hanging close to her full hips and the convex little curve of her belly.

Fargo peered at Bart Dodd. The man looked drawn, the lines in his face with an added deepness and a tiredness around his eyes. "You holding up?" Fargo asked quietly.

"Yes, yes, fine," the man said, too quickly, and Fargo made no comment. "Just haven't done much range riding in some while," the man added, aware of the big man's glance still probing. "Bobby's been handling that end of it on the ranch," Bart Dodd said.

"Ride your wagon for the afternoon. We don't need everyone now. Everything's going well," Fargo suggested.

"No, I'll be all right," Bart Dodd said, defensiveness quick in his voice. "Just got to get back in the swing of it." He strode off, pulled himself onto the thin horse with a show of spirit. Fargo felt Sandra Dodd beside him and she raised her glance to him as her husband rode off.

"Bart's not a well man, hasn't been for years," she said. "I'll try not to let him overdo."

"Overdoing is what it's all about here, which means he's really useless," Fargo said.

"You don't go in for understanding, do you?" she said with a touch of resentment.

"I go in for truth," he answered.

Her round face drew together. "That's still pretty harsh," she said softly.

"Not as harsh as this trip's going to get," he said. She didn't answer, climbed back onto the big California rack bed, snapped the reins, and drove away. Fargo remounted, passed the Sturdivents talking to Henrietta Baker. The old lady seemed far and away the freshest of all and Fargo went on, admiration for her growing inside him. She was one tough old bird. He rode from the herd, up on the distant low hilltops again, swept the terrain with a long, slow glance as Liz Ryan came along to halt beside him.

"Looking for the Haskells?" she asked.

"Not really," he said. "Just keeping a weather eye out for anything."

"Why not the Haskells?" she pressed.

"I'd guess he expects us to take the usual trail toward Abilene. When he finds out different he'll come looking for us," Fargo said, his eyes still moving over the land.

"Maybe he won't find us by then," she commented.

"Not likely," he grunted. "A blind man could pick up our trail. The only questions are when they'll make a move, where they'll do it, and what they'll try."

He started back down the hillside and she went with him. "So we just have to wait," she said.

"I didn't say that," he muttered.

"What else can we do?" She frowned.

He gave her a sharp glance. "You ask too damn many questions," he said.

"You give too damn few answers," she threw back, sent the bay into a canter, and rode off angrily as he laughed. He rode on to the front of the herd, by late afternoon had decided on the night patrols, four hands keeping watch over the herds, three shifts of three hours each. The night usually had a quieting effect on cattle. They just naturally stayed closer together but too many unexpected surprises could turn up. He'd learned that long ago. A watch was always needed and he made his choices for each of the shifts.

The rolling hills narrowed some and he waved the wagons on ahead of the herd as the cattle began to bunch together. The Downer boys, the Sturdivents, and Bobby Dodd drew up at the rear, pushing the herds forward and gathering up stragglers. Fargo rode forward, passed Sandra Dodd, and her glance had lost its resentment and he caught the hint of a smile. His eyes found Bart Dodd on the thin horse. The man had both hands on the saddle horn, his face tight as a pregnant sow's belly, and Fargo moved to his side.

"Get in your wagon," he said, an order delivered quietly but very definitely. Bart Dodd was willing to obey, Fargo saw, as the man dismounted at once and pulled himself onto the rear of the wagon where he sank down in exhaustion. Fargo frowned as he rode on, wondered if Bart Dodd would last even the first part of the trip. He passed Henrietta Baker. The woman gave him a brisk nod, her eyes bright and full of fire. He grinned at her and she understood and he rode on. He glanced back to watch the herds pulling together to pass through the slightly narrower land and turned forward again. The afternoon was fast drawing to a close. Cassie and Carrie had ridden ahead to the top of an incline and he saw them rein up, wave to him as one. He rode up to see the lone wagon a hundred yards on, the drive shafts hanging emptily, not a horse in sight.

Two women sat on the high driver's seat of the wagon, a flat-bed dray piled with boxes and trunks. They rose, waved excitedly, and he started toward them, Cassie and Carrie going with him. Liz Ryan caught up, joined in, and the other wagons crested the hill and followed. The women were on the ground as Fargo halted before them and swung from the saddle. They were both clad in gray cotton dresses, unshapely garments, both wore black hair pulled back tight around their heads and tied in a bun at the back, the severity giving their fairly young faces added years.

"Thank God," the one woman said. "Oh, thank God. We've been praying somebody would come by. I'm Amy White. This is my sister, Lois."

"What happened?" Fargo asked.

"Our horses just ran off last night," the first woman said. "We unhitched them and let them graze some and they just took off."

"Something must have spooked them," the other added. Fargo glanced up as the wagons came to a halt and others climbed down to gather around. "God, it's good to see all of you," the one called Lois said with a deep sigh of relief.

"Traveling all by yourselves?" Fargo heard Henrietta Baker ask.

"We always do," Amy White said.

"Where were you headed?" Fargo asked.

"Houndsville," the woman said. "That's a good fifty miles north. We were on our way to new work."

"Doing what?" Fargo questioned.

"Farming and some housework," the woman said. "We hire out, get good money for it. People pay when they need you." She glanced up at the darkening sky. "It'll be dark in another ten minutes. Could we spend the night with you good folks?" she asked apprehensively.

"Of course, my dears," Fargo heard Reverend Richards intone. "Of course you may."

Fargo turned a hard glance on the man. "If I say so," he cut in coldly. The Reverend met the ice in his eyes, swallowed, summoned a weak smile.

"Yes, yes, of course. I stand corrected. Mister Fargo is heading our drive," he said to the two women.

"Why couldn't they stay the night with us?" Fargo heard Liz ask.

"Indeed, you certainly wouldn't turn away from those in need," Reverend Richards added.

Fargo glanced at the two women, then back to the Reverend. "Wouldn't think of it," he said, his smile flashing with generous affability.

"Well, that's settled, then," the Reverend said to the two women. "And in the morning, we'll see to finding new horses for you. Come, my dears, you are welcome to whatever we have."

Fargo let the Reverend lead the two women off and met Liz Ryan's narrowed eyes as Henrietta Baker sat her horse alongside the girl. "Why the about-face?"

Liz asked. "You were going to say no, weren't you?"

Fargo looked injured. "You misjudge me," he protested.

"Hell, I do," Liz shot back.

"Let's say the Reverend made me see the light with a few good words." Fargo smiled and heard Henrietta Baker's laugh, glanced at the woman.

"You're somethin', Fargo," the old woman said with a toss of her white-haired head. "You're somethin', I'll give you that." She rode off still chuckling and he glanced at Liz, saw the green eyes narrowed.

"I agree with her, though I'm not sure what," the young woman snapped.

"You let me know soon as you decide." Fargo smiled and she turned away. He tied the pinto behind the chuck wagon and assigned the three shifts for the night. It was dark when he finished and he took a tin of beans and bacon from Barney McCall, perched against a low rock, and ate. The two women were nearby, sitting with the Reverend, and one glanced at him.

"We're beholden to you for taking us in," she said. "We were really growing desperate."

"I guess you were." Fargo smiled back, rose, and carried his plate to the water barrel. He'd just finished cleaning it off when two blond heads appeared, sidled up to him, their eyes bright with questions.

"You going to turn in early?" the one asked.

"Carrie?" he questioned.

"Cassie." She giggled.

"Well, are you?" the other demanded.

"Why?" Fargo returned.

"Just asking," Cassie said and her eyes gave the lie to the answer.

"Ask tomorrow night," he said, saw her face fall at once. He examined their faces, noses, eyebrows, lips, dimples, the way their hair fell along their necks. Not one damn thing to help tell them apart.

"Keep trying." Carrie laughed, reading his thoughts. "Tomorrow night," she said and they went off, wiggling in perfect symmetry. They were sure as hell far removed from Daddy's proper sanctimoniousness, Fargo pondered. Little teases? Or little adventuresses? He set the questions aside. Finding out might be fun. But he'd other questions on his mind now. He took his bedroll down, set it out at the edge of the small camp, checked the riders watching the herd, saw that Liz Ryan had bedded down inside the chuck wagon. He walked around the outer edge of the camp in the light of a half-moon, paused at the wagon belonging to the two women. When he moved on, he continued to circle the campsite, slowed as he saw Sandra Dodd's full figure step out from behind the big wagon. She wore a cotton nightdress and her full, billowy breasts pushed over the edge of the neckline and her hair hung loosened, reaching below her shoulders. She halted before him, dark-brown eyes looking up solemnly, and he could feel the banked sultriness of her. She wasn't pushing it at him, he knew that. It was simply there, held in for so long it vibrated of itself.

"Bart should rest tomorrow," she said. "He won't do it unless you make it an order."

"If we don't need him," Fargo said.

"You've enough hands for now. Things are going nicely," she said. "If he rests a day he'll be all right again."

"All right," he told her.

Her hand moved, hesitantly, touched his arm, drew back quickly. "Thank you," she said and the deep-brown eyes stayed on him.

"Tell me about him sometime," he said. "And about you."

She nodded. "Yes, sometime," she said. He watched her return to the wagon, heard her climb in from the other side. He went back to his bedroll, loosened his

80

gunbelt, and stretched out and listened to the sounds of the campsite grow dim. A few giggles from Cassie and Carrie carried through the night, a murmur of conversation from the Downer wagon, and finally only silence. Fargo closed his eyes, kept them closed, let himself almost fall asleep. Almost. He'd learned how to hang on the edge of sleep, a half-rest of its own, yet aware and awake to the slightest sound. He opened his eyes after a time, not because of a sound, but because it was time.

He reached into his shirt, patted an object there, rose silently, tightened his gunbelt, and moved from his bedroll. Once again he began to circle the campsite, this time silent as a puma on the prowl. Beyond the wagons, the dark mass of steers formed an almost solid expanse of blackness, low mooing sounds drifting across the silence. Fargo continued on along the edge of the campsite, circled sleeping bags with the Sturdivents inside them.

He was almost at the flat-bed dray belonging to the two women when he halted, caught the glint of white hair behind a line of bushes. He shifted direction, came up behind Henrietta Baker to close a big hand over her mouth. He kept it there as her head turned to look at him, no alarm in her eyes, and he drew his hand away. "What the hell are you doing?" he asked in a whisper.

"Watching. I was wondering when you'd show up," she said.

He dropped to one knee beside her, frowned at her. Henrietta's parchment face flashed a smile at him. "I'll be damned," he murmured.

"An old chicken gets to be a smart chicken," the woman whispered.

"Then stop clucking," Fargo ordered, settled down beside her, and shook his head again. He had only a few minutes to wait when he saw the two figures moving toward the wagon, bent over, stepping carefully. The first one, Amy, went to one of the boxes at the rear of the wagon. The other one joined her in lifting it as she dug beneath it for a hatbox, pulled it out, and raised the lid. She pushed her arm inside, groped around in the box, and Fargo heard her whispered oath as she continued to feel about inside the hatbox.

He rose, took two long strides on cat's feet, neither woman aware of his presence. "This what you're looking for?" he asked mildly.

The woman dropped the hatbox, whirled to face him, and the other spun around with her. Fargo pulled his hand from inside his shirt, pushed the tied bundle of firecrackers at the two women. They stared at it, slowly raised their eyes to him. The one called Lois panicked and started to bolt away but he had seen the fear leaping in her eyes, kicked out with one foot, and caught her leg as she tried to race off. She cried out as she went flying sideways, hitting the ground on one shoulder. He never took his eyes from the other one, was ready as she sprang at him, yanking the knife from inside her dress, a small close-range blade not more than two inches long. She ripped upward with it and Fargo ducked to the side, came down hard on her forearm, and she screamed. She screamed again as he twisted and the little knife flew out of her hand. He saw Henrietta Baker rush from the bushes to scoop it up as he yanked the woman around, holding her by one arm, pushed her forward as he grabbed the other one starting to pull herself to her feet.

He saw heads popping from wagons, forms hurrying outside as he propelled the two women into the center of the campsite. Reverend Richards, a long nightshirt covering his paunch, appeared and the twins behind him in identical pink gowns. "What's the meaning of all this?" the Reverend demanded, looked shocked. Fargo answered by spinning the two women, flinging them half-across the clearing. They fell sprawling on the ground.

"Stop that," the Reverend said and Fargo saw the others had all emerged from their wagons and bedrolls. He stepped forward, took hold of one woman's hair, and yanked hard.

"Ow, damn," she screamed but the tightly drawn black hair came off in his hand and a cascade of bottle-red curls fell down from her head. He flung her aside, yanked the wig from the other one, and she screamed, too, as her peroxide hair streamed out. Both women lay on the ground, breathing hard, glaring up at him. "Sonofabitch," the one spit out. Fargo's smile was made of ice. He pulled the bundle of firecrackers from his shirt, tossed them out for the others to see.

"Your poor stranded ladies were going to set them off," he bit out. "You know what that would have done, I expect." He saw Harry Sturdivent nod and Reverend Richards continue to stare at the two women. "It'd have stampeded the herd. They'd have come charging this way, smashing every wagon and trampling the rest of you into the ground. Maybe a few of you might've gotten away. Maybe."

"Wow," one of the twins gasped.

"Good Lord," the Reverend breathed.

Fargo saw Liz Ryan in a long shirt, her legs bare beneath it, slender and beautiful as a pair of marsh reeds. He let his eyes bore into her. She drew a deep sigh. "How'd you know?" she asked.

He grinned, turned to Henrietta Baker. "You want to tell them, Henrietta?" he asked. "You knew it, too."

The old lady chuckled. "Yep, saw it right away, same as Fargo did. Their hands, look at 'em. Farming and housework? Never, not with those hands. They haven't seen a hoe or a rake in years, if they ever did."

"Dancehall girl hands," Fargo said. "Creamed,

lotioned, and painted." He saw Amanda Koster watching, Sophie beside her. The big woman wore a burlap nightshirt, Sophie a cotton robe that didn't pull closed enough to hide full-figured legs and dimpled knees. "Hold on to the blond one," he told the woman and Amanda Koster stepped forward, yanked the girl up as though she were a feather, dragged her stumbling away. Fargo stepped to the one with the bottle-red hair, reached down, and lifted her to her knees with one big hand closed tight around the collar of her gray dress.

"Afterward, who was coming to get you?" he asked. She glared at him. He tightened his hand, saw the veins in her neck begin to stand out. "You can do this the easy way or the hard way." She continued to glare and he half-turned his hand. The veins in her neck began to throb and grow purple and he saw her breath become shallow. He watched the tiny points of fear form in her eyes. "You'd have pretty near killed everybody here. I don't give a damn if I kill you, honey," Fargo growled.

"Fargo," he heard the Reverend call.

"Go say a prayer for her, Reverend," Fargo snapped out, his eyes boring into the dancehall girl's face. He tightened his hand another turn. The fear had grown, filling her eyes now. He saw her try to talk, fight to emit a strained, half-strangled sound. He released his grip. "Where and when. Talk," he rasped.

She swallowed, regained her voice. "A half-hour after," she said through hoarse vocal chords.

He released his grip, motioned to Harry Sturdivent. "Tie and gag her. Put her with the other one," he ordered. He turned, saw Henrietta Baker watching, and the old woman winked at him. "You've made me eat words, Henrietta," he said. "I wish I'd ten more antiques like you along." The woman tossed her white-haired head back and laughed as she strolled away. "Go back to sleep," he told the others. "It's over."

Liz Ryan, lovely legs pale in the half-light, the long shirt reaching midthigh, watched him critically. "You're not turning in," she said.

"Unfinished business. They were going to wait a half-hour. That means they're not far, near enough to hear the sound of the firecrackers," he said.

"That's why you decided to let them stay. You noticed their hands and figured to be ready and waiting for their move. I'm sorry I pushed at you, earlier," she said.

"You are setting a hell of a record for being wrong," he commented. Her mouth tightened at once and she turned, started back to the chuck wagon. "But you've got nice legs," he called after her, saw her slow for an instant, hurry on without glancing back.

He strode to the pinto, had just finished tightening the cinch when Cassie and Carrie appeared in their pink gowns. They made him think he had double vision, he muttered silently. Their pretty faces were aglow with eager curiosity. "Would you have killed her if she hadn't answered?" the one asked.

"She answered," he said harshly. "That's all that counts. Get the hell to sleep," he ordered. They turned obediently, hurried off together, ripe, young bodies moving sinuously under the pink gowns. He added ghoulish curiosity to their traits. They were young enough for it, he grunted to himself, swung onto the pinto, and headed from the campsite. He paused at Ed Norbert as the man rode watch along the far side of the herd.

"All quiet," Norbert said. "No problems." Fargo grunted a nod and rode off. He headed north. Haskell's boys wouldn't be behind them and not in front. The hills were a little steeper and closer north. It seemed the most likely direction. He rode hard for five minutes, slowed to a walk when he began to crest the rises of the series of small hills. His logic proved right as he reined up behind a stand of little-hip haw-thorns with their clusters of little white flowers. Two horses rested just below, their forms clear in the dim half-moon. He squinted, found the shapes of the two men nearby, both seated on the ground. A tiny glow flickered in the dark. One was smoking. Fargo dismounted, drew the big Sharps from its saddle case, pushed it back in again. The light was too poor to shoot from this distance.

He unholstered the Colt .45 and began to move down the gradual slope, staying at the edge of the trees. The two men took shape more clearly, one with a wide-brimmed Stetson, the one smoking hatless. Fargo edged closer until the tree line came to an end. Twenty yards or so separated him from the men.

"What the hell's taking them so long?" he heard one of them growl.

Fargo leveled the Colt at the one with the Stetson. He wanted questions answered if possible. "The party's over," he called out. "Don't move."

He saw the two figures stiffen, the one with the cig-arette sit up straight. They peered toward him, trying to pick out his figure. He stayed in the trees, called out again, his voice soft. "Get up, nice and slow," he ordered. The one with the hat frowned in the direc-tion of his voice. Slowly, he started to push himself upward, pressing both hands on the ground, when the push became a lunging dive as the man catapulted himself sideways toward a big rock. Fargo's finger had but to tighten on the trigger and the Colt exploded a shot instantly. The man's diving figure seemed to flatten out, not unlike a bird coming in to land on the ground, slammed into the dirt, and lay still. The second one was rolling, yanking his gun out, firing wildly. Fargo heard the shots hit a tree six feet from where he stood. The man came up on his feet, started to race for the horses as he continued to fire, trying to lay down his own cover. His shots crashed into the trees, disappeared into bushes. He had just reached the horse, started to vault into the saddle when Fargo fired, the figure in his sights. The man hung against the horse for a moment, one hand clutching the saddle horn as his body shuddered with the impact of the bullet. The back of his neck, just across the shoulder blades, spurted red, and he slowly slid from the side of the horse, only his hand gripped around the saddle horn holding him for a moment longer, and then that, too, slid away. He crumpled into a heap almost under the horse.

Fargo moved forward, holstering the Colt, stared at the two men, and turned away. The entire business had given him one answer. Haskell wasn't waiting along the Abilene Trail. He'd tried his first move, a neat one if it had worked, a stampede with nobody much left to make accusations, certainly nobody with proof of anything. Fargo walked back to the pinto. Haskell would move again, of course, but not for a few days. He'd have to regroup, find a place, plan his move. Blakelock Haskell did the thinking, Fred Haskell the doing, Fargo was certain. A two-headed snake. He half-laughed at the thought, rode back to camp slowly, letting his own countermoves form in his mind. They had been lucky this time. It'd get rougher. He reached the campsite, managed to get in three hours of good sleep before the dawn came to wake him. He woke, was ready to ride again as the others began to stir themselves. He allowed time for breakfast and Amanda Koster came to him, the two women in tow, hands tied and mouths gagged.

"Take the gags off," he told her. Sophie came along, blond braids hanging down over deep breasts that were barely contained by another peasant blouse with a square neck.

"What do you want me to do with them?" Amanda

Koster asked and he caught a hint of anticipation in her eyes.

"Just tie them in their wagon," Fargo said, saw the light leave her eyes.

"That's all?" she asked.

"That's all," he said. He looked at the two women. "You're friends won't be coming for you," he said.

Alarm seized their faces at once. "You can't just leave us tied in that damn wagon," the one protested.

"When nobody shows up, Haskell will come looking. He'll find his boys and then you two," Fargo said.

"What if he doesn't?" the woman said.

Fargo shrugged coldly. "It'll teach you not to play with firecrackers," he said. "Tie them."

The big woman dragged the two back, holding them as if they were wriggly dolls, and he watched Sam Sturdivent help her tie them in the wagon. Sophie's eyes were on him and he met her glance. "I like a man who's not afraid to be hard," she said, her pink cheeks glowing. She stepped closer, her bright eyes moving over him almost possessively. "You are not like any man I have ever met," she said, her accent faint.

"*Sophie!*" The voice cut through the air sharply, Amanda Koster's deep voice, and he saw the woman frowning. "I'm waiting for you, Sophie," she barked and the girl turned, hurried to her, fell in step beside the big woman. Fargo tabled thoughts in a corner of his mind, saddled the pinto, and moved out as the Downer boys started to push the herd forward. The twins waved at him as they rode herd on the other side and he saw Liz pass, chasing after a yearling intent on straying off by itself.

He rode forward into the new day and wished the Haskells were all that lay between them and New Mexico.

6

The herd moved with bawling and bellowing obedience and he saw Sandra Dodd approach on the thin horse. Her hair, freshly combed, glistened in the morning sun and her brown eyes met his glance and she half-smiled. "You didn't need me, I see," he remarked.

"Bobby's driving the wagon. Bart's resting inside. He's got one of his bad days. Too much effort yesterday," she said.

"Ride a piece with me. Talk," Fargo said and she fell in beside him.

"It's some kind of blood condition, the doctor said. It started six years ago. He gets tired after any kind of heavy exertion. It's been getting worse."

"Why'd he come on the drive?" Fargo questioned.

She shrugged. "Stubbornness. His pride. He wants Bobby to look up to him."

"Bobby giving trouble on that?"

"No, it's all in Bart's mind. Bobby understands. He's a good kid. It's been hard on him, having to do a man's work, growing up," Sandra said.

"And you, has it been hard on you?"

A rueful smile edged her lips. "Yes, but differently. More than I knew," she said.

"Meaning what?" he questioned.

"Coming on the drive, riding here with you, it's made it all harder suddenly," she said and his eyes questioned. "Staying on the ranch, mostly alone with Bart and Bobby, it was like being in sort of a convent.

You get to live with what you don't have. You get to handle it because you have no choice. But out here, it all comes rushing back over you. Needing, wanting, feeling, it all comes alive again and it's a burning inside you." She paused, her brown eyes boring into him, a frown clouding her face, suddenly vibrant, full lips slightly parted. "I ought to feel guilty, but dammit, I don't," she said. "I feel like I've been cheated out of something that ought to have been my right."

"How long's it been?" Fargo asked quietly.

"Six years, since he took sick," the woman said. "Not his fault. No blame on him. But that doesn't help any." She half-laughed suddenly, a nice sound. "Why'd I tell you all this? Why'd I feel you'd understand?" she said.

"Same reason I figured you'd tell me," he said. She let another rueful smile touch her face and he felt the simmering of her. She nodded, saying everything with the motion, turned her horse away, and rode back to the herd. Fargo moved on, circled, watched the Downer boys work the far edge of the herd, approved of what he saw and rode on ahead. He moved on to cross an arid stretch of land that went to the horizon line. His eyes moved constantly, sweeping the horizon in all directions. He heard the sound of a horse behind him, turned in the saddle to see Liz Ryan, her slender figure almost severe, made of angles and everything understated and yet she sent out her own brand of femaleness, a kind of bristly sex. She pulled up beside him with a glance, disdained words. He let her ride in silence which ended when he halted, pointed to a set of tracks on the dry ground.

"Haskell?" she asked.

"No," he said. "Indian ponies. Squaws following on foot. Pawnee, most likely."

"Any sign of Haskell?" she asked as they went on.

"Not yet," he answered.

"So far so good, then," she said. Fargo grunted, a derisive sound. "Don't you ever look on the bright side of things?" she asked sharply.

"Ask me when this is over," he said. His eyes went down to the arid ground. "Lousy cattle country. Nothing but scrub brush and shadscale. No grazing land," he muttered.

"This the way it's all going to be?" she asked.

"For another day or so. Then we'll be into good grasslands again," he said. "But everything has its good side." She frowned at the remark. "Haskell won't make a move here. The land's too open."

She nodded, rode on in silence until she decided to make the comment, taking care to keep her voice casual. "I saw Sandra Dodd riding with you before," she said. "Sandra's a lonely woman."

"Thanks for the warning." He grinned.

"It wasn't a warning, just an observation," she said haughtily.

"Bullshit." He smiled back, met her glare. "Just one question. You warning me for her sake or yours?"

He watched the brown-flecked green eyes widen in instant anger. "Not everybody's Blanche Haskell," she threw back. "Some of us have principles."

"They can sure get in the way, can't they?" he said.

She opened her mouth, snapped it closed, and spun the bay around to gallop away. Fargo rode on calmly, halted when he came to a broad, shallow gulley filled with slow-moving but clear water. He dismounted, sat down, and waited until the others came along. The herd made for the water, pushing and bellowing. "Spread them out along the banks," he ordered and the cowhands moved the herd out to avoid their trampling each other. The cattle slaked their thirst along a quarter-mile of the gulley and Fargo let them take all they wanted. Finally he remounted. "Move 'em on," he called. "We'll bring them together on the other side."

He helped his range riders chase the steers across the gulley and then herd them back into a manageable unit on the other side. Henrietta Baker chased down three stubborn steers with him, hooting and waving a black cape until they moved back into the herd. She pulled up beside him, her eyes crackling bright in the parchment face. "What'd you say to Liz Ryan before? She came back looking mad enough to bite a rattler."

Fargo laughed. "Touched a tender spot, I guess," he said.

"That's always dangerous, young feller," she said. "Specially with these young girls. I see they've all got eyes for you. Better be careful." She laughed and rode off happily.

Fargo kept the herd moving until almost nightfall and then had them gathered into a loose circle on the arid land just beneath a low incline. He rotated the order for the night shifts but kept the men and the Downer boys as the base patrols. Barney McCall handed him a plate of rabbit stew as he sat down for a meal and Liz came over. "How long are you going to head west?" the man asked.

"Till I turn south," Fargo answered calmly.

The man cast a slightly nervous glance at Liz. "I was wondering, that's all," he said.

"Dammit, Barney, ask him. We're paying him," Liz snapped. Fargo raised his eyes to her, fastened her with a waiting stare that held the edge of frost in it. "It seems we're taking the long way when we could be moving south by now," she said. "I think Haskell's decided to back off."

"You want your money back?" Fargo said quietly. "I'll ride out tonight."

She was taken aback, an answer she hadn't expected

and he saw alarm leap into her eyes. "Dammit, Liz," Barney McCall cut in. "You and that sharp tongue of yours. Don't pay her no mind, Fargo. You're boss. That's enough for me," he said placatingly. Fargo held the girl in his stare and abruptly Liz spun on her heel and stalked away, fury in the sharp tattoo of her boots on the dry ground. "Damn, I don't know what's pushing at that girl," her uncle said.

Fargo kept his smile inside himself. "She's just naturally suspicious, maybe," Fargo said blandly.

"I can't figure it," the man said, shook his head, and returned to the chuck wagon. Fargo finished the meal, watched the others begin to settle in for the night. The twins passed him, flashed a bright smile that said more than it seemed. He watched them disappear into the Reverend's wagon, walked to the pinto, and moved from the camp. He rode up onto the incline that rose to the left, halted near the top, and looked down at the herd and the circle of wagons nearby. He laid out his bedroll and undressed to his underpants, stretched out, and watched the stars sprinkle themselves across the warm night. An occasional bellow drifted up from the herd below and, arms behind his head, he waited. His ears picked up the sound after an hour had passed, soft steps, a horse being walked slowly. He watched as the shape emerged from the darkness, moving up the incline, a single horse and two riders.

Twin blond heads, almost silver in the half-moon, peered at him over the horse's head, slid down from the animal. No saddle, he noted, smiled to himself. They both wore ponchos, and, from below the edge of the ponchos, the pink of their gowns peaked. They came over to him, their eyes taking in the contours of his hard-muscled body, the powerful shoulders and the long, tapering torso, the mound pushing out in his pants. They sank to their knees beside him, eyes bright, tiny smiles holding their lips.

"I wondered," he said softly.

"Whether we'd be coming?" one asked.

"No," he said. They frowned. "Whether you'd be coming alone or together," he said. They smiled. "Your daddy wouldn't be happy about your coming up here," Fargo said.

"No, he wouldn't, but then Daddy wouldn't be happy about a lot of things we've done," the one said.

"You telling me you're women of the world?" Fargo poked at them.

They giggled in unison. "I guess not. But we've tried. That's why we had to come up here to see you," the other said.

"What's that mean?" Fargo asked, turned to rest on one elbow. "Cassie?" he asked.

"Carrie," she said. "It means Daddy used to be a traveling preacher and he'd take us along. On Sunday square-dance parties we'd find a boy we liked and get him to go into the woods with us."

"It never worked right," Cassie said, making a face. "They were always afraid. They'd go halfway and then nothing more would happen. They were boys, just boys."

"The right church but the wrong pew," Carrie quipped and they both giggled.

"There are some things you ought to try alone," Fargo suggested.

"Yes, I guess so, but another time," Cassie said. With one quick motion, she whipped the poncho over her head, began to unbutton the pink gown. Carrie did the same and Fargo watched as they shook off the gowns, his eyes moving from one to the other with undisguised admiration. The round, young breasts were just as high and thrusting as they seemed under clothes, exactly the same, both pairs standing out, firm

94

and full of youthful vigor. Very pink nipples, flat, virginal, with equally pink, small circles around each. Identical in every respect. Both had small, tucked-in waists and little rounded bellies that curved out deliciously. His eyes moved down to their pubic mounds, both faintly swelling, the blond triangles exactly alike in size and shape. Kneeling before him, they both vibrated with eager, almost exploding desire. Not a mole, not a blemish, not a line or mark anywhere to tell them apart, he noted with amazement.

Cassie leaned forward and opened her mouth on his, her high breasts' soft points pressing into his chest. She half-rolled over him and he turned with her, grasped her breasts with his hand, caressed both. "Oh, God, yes, oh, Fargo," she breathed. He felt Carrie's hands on his back, pressing, caressing, the touch of her breasts against him as she pressed herself against him. Cassie's little belly was lifting up to his and he felt her legs moving to open, spreading wide. His mouth found her breast, pulled one, then the other. "Eeeaaahhhh . . ." she gasped and Carrie's hands were moving up and down his legs, as though she were trying to memorize every part of him by touch.

Cassie pushed upward and he felt the wiry triangle rubbing against him. He was ready for her, eager, carried along by the fervent, unvarnished desire both exploded. He touched the tip of her rounded lips and she half-screamed, thrust herself up, half-enveloping him with her warm portal. He moved into her, felt Carrie half-wrapped around his leg, stroking, clinging, making little sounds. Cassie's lips fell open and she gasped out the words. "Oh, shit, oh, wow, oh, shit, yes, yes . . . oh, Jesus." She cried out in a moment of pain as he thrust all the way in but laughter was in the pain and she clung to him. He felt Carrie's cheek pressed against his buttocks as he moved back and forth in Cassie. Gasps and cries, both laced with sheer joy, almost laughter, came from Cassie and he moved faster with her as she pushed up and down. Her sheer joy enveloped him, showered a youthful eagerness over him as she pushed a breast up for his mouth. "Yes, oh, damn, yes," she cried out as he took it. He felt her begin to quiver, lunge upward. "Oh, oh, oh, oh, shit . . . oh, my God, my God," she cried out with each quivering thrust and then the words turned into a long, wailing cry that ended in a half-shout and her arms clung around his neck. "Wheeeeeee . . . oh, damn, woooooooow," she cried out, let herself fall back.

Fargo felt Carrie's hands on him, groping, forgotten for the moment, now finding his still-ready, vibrant maleness. "Me, now, oh, me, Fargo, please, please," she demanded, pulled him around to her. He saw her legs lift, fall out, and come together, hitting his waist, sliding down to his hips. She pushed against him, seeking with desperate eagerness with her little mound firm, opened wide, pushing hard, and he lifted, found her, sank into her, and she screamed for an instant and the scream became a cry of pure delight.

"Shit, oh, God almighty, oh, boy, oh, damn." He heard her half-laughing as she pumped against him, her words an echo of Cassie's. Dimly, he heard Cassie moaning softly, a cooing sound beside him, and he was aware of her one hand stroking his hip gently. "Yes, oh, yes, more, oh, damn more," Carrie was gasping out and she moved furiously up and down, young legs driving her torso in short, pistonlike motions, her heels dug into the ground. He felt himself ready to explode, managed to hold back until her torso arched upward and the crying, laughing wail of pure pleasure took wing. She pulsated wildly as her body stayed arched, quivering, and he felt the throbbing spasms of her against his organ, the life-breath of ecstasy, sweet silent clutchings, and then she fell back onto the bedroll.

"Oh . . . oh, ooooh," she sighed, a long, heart-felt gasp, as he drew from her, rolled to lay beside her. He felt Cassie's warm full breasts press against him as she came to lie half-over him at once, her lips nibbling along his chest. Carrie turned, covered the other half of him, let her lips play across his shoulders and down the side of his pectoral muscles.

"It was everything, Fargo," he heard Carrie murmur.

"Everything," Cassie echoed.

"For starters," Fargo commented. "You'll learn how to take it slower."

Carrie nodded, bit the tip of his ear. Cassie rubbed her face against his chest. "We had to explode," she murmured. "All those false starts for so long."

She lifted her head, gazed at him, and Carrie did the same. "It was worth all of them, though," Carrie said. "God, it's great, better than we hoped."

"It'll get better, too," Cassie said and he nodded. He saw them watch the smile that moved across his face. He'd found how to tell them apart. Cassie was tighter, Carrie throbbed more violently. "What are you smiling about?" Carrie asked.

"I know how to tell you apart, now," he said blandly.

They frowned at him, looked rueful, then, realization filtering through, they giggled, broke into laughter. They exchanged a smug glance. "That's all right," Cassie said. "That won't help you most times."

He peered back and it was his turn for a touch of ruefulness. They were right, dammit, he muttered silently. He watched them take the pink gowns, wriggle into them, each movement a cry of eager youthful joy, absolutely without pretense. "We'd best be getting back," Cassie said. They leaned forward, kissed him on each cheek, drew the ponchos over themselves, and swung onto the horse. They waved, looked totally contented as they rode away to disappear into the night. Fargo lay back on the bedroll, listened to the sound of a distant coyote, finally slept.

The morning came to wake him and he washed with the water from his canteen, dressed, and rode down the incline to the wagons. Barney had coffee on and he saw the others gathered around the thin line of steam rising from the heavy, battered enamel coffeepot. He'd almost reached the wagons when Liz cut across on the bay to meet him, green eyes narrowed, peering hard at him.

"Cassie and Carrie rode in late last night," she said sharply.

"You out riding alone again?" he asked.

"No, I just couldn't sleep. I was awake and saw them slip into camp on one horse," she said. "They'd been to see you, hadn't they?"

Fargo's eyebrows lifted. "Yes, not that it's any of your damn business," he said mildly.

Her eyes flashed. "It is my business. My uncle hired you. They're only sixteen and the Reverend's daughters."

"And you're no nursemaid, sweetie." Fargo smiled. "They wanted to talk. They wanted some pointers."

"About what?" she snapped.

"Bull-riding," he said casually. She was still staring at him, anger and uncertainty mixed in her eyes, as he rode on with a polite tip of his hat. He swung from the saddle, took a mug of coffee from Barney McCall, and walked to where Henrietta Baker, Ed Norbert, Billy Walsh, and the Downer boys were congregated. His eyes swept the sky where a layer of low stratus clouds gathered on the horizon.

"I'm going to step up the pace today. I want us in Colorado Territory by night," he told them.

"Any special reason?" Ed Norbert asked.

Fargo nodded to the distant horizon. "Rain, maybe. If it comes hard it'll turn this dirt land into a sea of mud. You know what that'll mean. The steers will use up a week's strength pulling their way in it," he said. "I want to be in grasslands if it hits us. That'll mean driving them hard and herding them tight."

"We can do it," Ed Norbert said.

"Pass the word along," Fargo ordered and watched Henrietta Baker swing onto her horse with supple ease. Sophie sauntered up to him in another of her peasant blouses. She had the two blond braids pulled forward so each rested on one ample breast.

"You like?" she said, running her fingers over the embroidery along the top of the blouse, pressing the fabric smooth across her breasts.

He wasn't sure which she meant, blouse or bosom. "I sure do," he said, taking care of whichever it was. She smiled almost coyly.

"Maybe you ride with me later?" she asked.

"Maybe," he said and watched her saunter off toward the wagon. As she reached it, Amanda Koster appeared, threw him a hard glance, and he heard her growl something at the girl, her broad, flat face darkened. He saw Sophie return a sulky pout as she snapped the reins and sent the seed-bed wagon rolling on. Fargo mounted the pinto, moved forward, and drew to a halt as the twins waved at him from the wagon, the Reverend just clambering into the driver's seat.

"Morning, Fargo," one called out with a happy giggle.

"What a great morning," the other added, beamed at him. Cassie and Carrie swung up on their mounts as the Reverend nodded at Fargo.

"The girls are certainly enjoying this drive. I've never seen them so happy," the Reverend said. "But then we know why, don't we?"

Fargo felt his eyebrows shoot skyward as he cast a quick glance at the minister. "We do?" he said cautiously.

"Of course," the Reverend answered. "A merry heart maketh a cheerful countenance. Book of Proverbs." He finished. "That's what I always say."

Fargo nodded, cast a glance at the twins, and rode on. He'd gone only a dozen yards when they caught up to him, giggling. "What do you always say?" Cassie laughed.

"A merry screw maketh a cheerful pussy. Book of Fargo," he answered.

"Does it ever," they chortled and rode on.

He wheeled the pinto in a half-circle, saw Bart Dodd clambering onto the thin horse, Bobby on his mount nearby and Sandra glowering up at him. They were having words, angry but kept low, and he heard the woman's voice suddenly rasied. "Go on, be a fool. Play hero," she snapped, whirled and climbed onto the big rack-bed wagon. Bart Dodd rode off and Bobby followed him. Fargo waited a moment, hung back, made his way alongside the wagon as the woman started off, her round face dark with anger.

"You've got to give him some rein," he remarked.

"I don't care for myself. It's Bobby I'm thinking of. I don't want him seeing his father collapse," she said angrily.

"I'll keep an eye on Bart," Fargo said.

Her eyes grew quieter, the anger fading from them. "Thanks, I'd be grateful," she said. He moved from her, rode on ahead, left the herd, and trotted across the scrubby ground until he could make out the land beginning to change, tufts of grass appearing. He glanced at the sky, watched the clouds moving nearer, and yet it was still a question of which way they'd blow. He went on slowly, let the herd catch up. The riders were doing a good job, driving them hard, and he saw the Downer boys, Norbert, Walsh, and Tom Sewall handling the rear of the herd, pressing them tight. Henrietta Baker held the right flank along with the twins. Amanda Koster rode the left with Bobby Dodd and Fargo circled the pinto as he saw Bart Dodd take off after a dozen steers that decided to break out. At least twenty yards away, yet, Fargo shouted to Bart Dodd.

"Easy, there," he called to the man. "Hold up a spell. Wait for back-up."

"I can handle it," the man yelled back and charged at the dozen steers. Fargo spurred the pinto on, swept the others, cursing softly. Amanda Koster was needed where she was, holding the left flank with Bobby. Dammit, Fargo swore under his breath as he saw Bart Dodd rush the steers. He saw three steers spin, their heads going down. Instantly, the others followed. Bart Dodd should have kept circling, backed away enough, nudging and hollering at their flanks. Instead, he charged at them, whirling his lariat. Fargo sent the pinto into a gallop as he saw the steers make one swing of their heads and charge. An expert rangehand wouldn't have been that close, and if he had he'd have known to turn off in a tight swerve. Bart Dodd reined up, tried to turn, but too late. The dozen steers slammed into his horse just as Fargo reached him. He saw the man fall, go down into the rushing, trampling steers.

He caught a glimpse of the man's form on the ground as he slammed the pinto into three steers from the side. They bellowed, broke away, and he had a chance to leap to the ground, pulling the heavy Sharps rifle from the saddle holster as he jumped. He landed a foot from Bart Dodd, a red-eyed steer starting for him. He slammed the rifle stock into the steer's snout and the animal bellowed, turned off. Fargo swung the rifle at two more, caught the end of

101

the tender noses, and they broke away. Out of the corner of his eye he glimpsed Ed Norbert and Billy Walsh arrive to drive the steers off and he whirled as a last, stubborn bull-calf decided to charge him, moving with exploding speed. With no room or time to swing the rifle, he tossed it aside, twisted away from one long horn that tried to hook him, and leaped forward, hands closing around the two horns. He dug heels into the dry ground, twisted hard on the horns, using the power of his shoulder muscles. Rodeo fashion, he wrestled the steer to the ground, slammed into the dirt with it, and let go, whirling to the side and regaining his feet. The bull-calf bleated, all the fight out of it, stumbled onto its feet, and moved off docilely.

Fargo let Norbert and Walsh herd it away as he dropped to one knee beside Bart Dodd. Miraculously, he hadn't been trampled except for some bruises and a torn shirt. But he was breathing shallowly in near shock and Fargo lifted him up as Sandra Dodd braked the wagon to a skidding halt. He set the man in the rear of it, Bobby anxiously helping to pull him inside. "He's lucky," Fargo said. "He could've been stomped into dust."

Sandra Dodd nodded gravely and Henrietta Baker appeared with a big blanket. "Keep this on him. Shock victims need to be kept warm," the old woman said. Sandra sat in the wagon with the man, fixed the blanket around him as Bobby climbed onto the driver's seat, took the reins. Bart Dodd's face was ghost-white, Fargo noted, but he breathed evenly.

"Move on," Fargo said to Bobby and the boy's face, grave and pale, set itself and he started the wagon forward. "Keep 'em moving," Fargo ordered the others. "Nothing more to be done here." He turned, rode ahead of the herd, chased a yearling back into place, and the drive began to move on. Bobby, driving slowly, pulled up behind the chuck wagon in last place. Henrietta Baker came alongside him and Fargo saw the hard-bitten approval in her eyes.

"You're everything they said you were," she said.

"Maybe a little worse," he allowed and she laughed as she turned back to the line of cattle. The day had passed by quickly. Fargo watched the grass beginning to thicken underfoot as dusk brought its purple grayness down on the land. "Keep moving," he called out and led the way, kept moving as darkness fell. The grass grew heavier and he felt the land start upward, spurred the pinto on up a slow hill to halt at the top. The sky was moonless, the night too dark to see much, but he made out the darker shapes of hilly land on both sides. He turned, rode back to the others, and felt the rain begin to fall, a light, cooling rain, and ordered them to make camp. The herd was gathered to the right of the wagons, the steers happily content to graze on the new grass. Fargo halted at the Dodd wagon. Sandra sat on the lowered tailgate, her dark eyes wide. Bart Dodd, covered with the blanket, lay hard asleep in the wagon. Fargo saw her eyes on him, round and deep with pain.

"You're a good man, Fargo. You didn't have to do it," she said.

"Do what?" he questioned.

"Risk your neck for him," she answered.

"Maybe I didn't do it for him," Fargo said and her deep eyes stayed on him. "Maybe I did it for you and the boy." She didn't answer but her eyes stayed on him. "He should've waited for back-up," Fargo said. "But he was showing off."

"I know," she said, her face taking on a touch of bitterness. "And he put your life on the line. That wasn't right."

"Right?" Fargo echoed. "Maybe not, but the truth is that we do a lot of things that aren't right, 'specially when we're driven to it." He turned the pinto and went on and felt her eyes following him. He swung from the saddle beside the chuck wagon where Barney McCall dished out a plate of stewed hen for him.

"Extra helping," Barney said with a smile. "You've earned it." Fargo didn't protest, moved off and leaned against a tree as he ate, looked up to see Liz coming toward him with her own plate. She halted in front of him, speared him with a probing appraisal.

"What makes you tick, Fargo?" she asked. "You're thoroughly unprincipled. You seem to have no moral conscience at all and then you do something like this afternoon. It's as though you're two different people."

"That's it," he said at once. "Two for the price of one. You pay your money and you take your pick."

"Why can't you just be the nice one?" She frowned.

"It's too hard." He grinned, finished his meal, and took his plate to the cleansing barrel. He took the pinto and walked on, aware that Liz's eyes followed him. The rain continued, a light drizzle, and he swung into the saddle, rode halfway up the hill in front of the campsite, and spread his bedroll. In the distance, he saw the flash of lightning and heard the faraway thunder. The main part of the storm had passed them and he undressed to his underpants, let the cool drops of rain soothe his body. He lay back, his mind turning. It was time to go over options, make plans and alternate plans. Haskell would make his next move soon. The man was being patient. He'd failed one try and he didn't want to bungle another. Patience equaled clever. It meant caution, not backing off. He had been sensing that Liz Ryan wasn't the only one who'd begun to believe Haskell had decided to back off. Fargo grunted, a grim sound.

The land would change character now, easier on cattle and horses, grass-covered softness and more water. But hills and plenty of tree cover. The bad with the good, he grunted to himself. He continued to play with plans in his head and the light rain had almost stopped when he heard the footsteps. The big Colt was in his hand instantly and he rolled to one elbow, his every muscle taut. But the footsteps were without stealth and he let his body relax as he saw the figure appear from the darkness to halt before him.

Sandra Dodd's deep eyes held at the virile beauty of his near-naked form for a long moment and then moved to his face as she stepped closer. He held her eyes, his face set. "You come to be grateful?" he said quietly. "You can go back, then. There's no need for that."

She shook her head slowly. "No, not to be grateful," she said, her voice tight. She drew a deep breath that pressed the billowy breasts tight against her white shirt. "I came because I'm near to exploding," she said, her voice finding strength. "I came because I can't hold back anymore. All these years, I've accepted, understood, taken my lot and held to it. I've done my abiding, but I can't do it anymore. I can't be locked up inside anymore."

Fargo nodded. "Why me? Why not one of the others, Norbert or Walsh?"

"They'd take it for more than it is or make me into less than I am," she said. "You understand."

"That all?" he pressed.

"They'll be around when this is over. You won't," she said.

Fargo gave her a slow smile. No dishonesty in her but a terrible need and resentment, a bitterness at life, at the cards dealt her. She had reason. She'd paid her dues. She deserved more and the throbbing need in her was suddenly as strong as the earth beneath him, her lips parted, her round, pleasantly pretty face flushed. He reached out, touched her shoulder, pulled gently. She trembled and fell onto him with an anguished cry, "Oh, Jesus, Fargo," the words tearing from her. Her hand ripped the blouse open and the large breasts burst out, came against his skin. "Oh, Jesus, Jesus, oh, yes," she groaned.

She tore the rest of the blouse off, pushed the loose skirt from her, and in seconds her nakedness was against his. Full, fleshy hips, rounded thighs, and a surprisingly tiny little triangle, her skin soft, smooth as silk. Her mouth crushed his, her tongue a wild and darting thing, and her hands swept over his body with a franticness. "Take me, Fargo, take me, please, please," she cried into his shoulder and lifted herself to push the billowy breasts against his face. He felt her fingers forming fists, little poundings against his ribs, opening and closing, opening again to move down his body until her right hand came to his waiting maleness. "Oooooh, God, ooooooh," she cried out as she clutched at him. He moved, pressed her onto her back and felt her hand pulling at him, drawing him into the wet roundness of her. "Please, please, Fargo, take me, oh, my God, take me," she cried out. Her belly rose against his, the little triangle not at all wiry. He held back and she screamed out her wanting, pushed against his tip and he moved into her slowly.

"Uh . . . uuuuuuuuh . . . oh, oh . . . oh . . . ," the sounds running together as though she could no longer find words, only long moans of consuming pleasure. He buried his face into her breasts and she clutched his head there, held him tight against her. He felt her legs pushing around him and her hips worked with him, the frenzied anxiety now translated into a surprisingly slow pace. She moved up and down in gentle rhythm and the moaning sounds were long, endless cries. He moved with her, let her set the pace, and realized her terrible wanting had become a fervent prolonging. When she felt herself losing control, her hands dug into him and he felt her try to hold back. "No, no, not yet, oh, no," she cried out, twisted her hips, tried to stay what could not be stayed any more than time could be held back.

Her gasp was a gutteral thing and he felt her contract around him as he came with her, the ecstasy so deep she could only choke out the strained sounds. She continued to clutch his face into her breasts until the terrible need had drained from her, for the moment at least, and she lay back and he heard the deep breath escape her. He lifted himself, lay beside her, enjoyed the full womanly shape of her with the tiny little triangle seeming out of place. Her deep eyes, grave and dark, held his gaze. "Once more, before I go back. Once more, please, Fargo," she said. "It'll have to last me some."

"Another six years?" he asked.

"No, I couldn't do that again. But I don't know how long," she said honestly. Her arms went around him and she pressed one breast against his lips. "Memory is a liar," she said with bitterness. "It doesn't hold a candle to the real thing." She reached for him, shuddered with pleasure as she touched him, and he felt the terrible need sweeping over her again. Contagious, it was, absolutely contagious. He took her again and let her fill the dark night with all the moaning ecstasy she'd been denied for too long.

It was later when she dressed, held him for another moment, that she kissed him tenderly. "Maybe once more, before the drive ends?" she said.

"Maybe," he allowed and watched her go down the hillside till she was out of sight. He pulled on underpants, stretched out on the bedroll. Not a good deed. He'd enjoyed himself too much to call it that. But not a bad one, either. He closed his eyes, had almost dropped off to sleep when he heard the sound of the hoofbeats, a lone horse moving fast up the hillside. Instinctively, his hand closed around the Colt beside his head, brought it up, and waited. He let the gunbarrel down only when he saw the slender figure rein up before him, leap from the bay to advance on him with fists clenched.

"You ought to be ashamed of yourself," she spit out in fury.

"You ought to stop your late-night spying," he said.

"I wasn't up spying. I saw Sandra Dodd leave the camp and start up here. I thought perhaps she just wanted to thank you again for this afternoon. I thought she'd be back in a few minutes. I guess I didn't want to believe anything else," Liz Ryan fumed. Fargo got to his feet and her eyes flicked across the hard-muscled, long, lean body. "Put something on, dammit. Haven't you any decency?"

"I've got something on," he said.

Her eyes flung fury at him. "You stop at nothing to indulge your appetite, do you? Impressionable sixteen-year-olds and now a distraught, vulnerable woman."

"You can be wrong even when you're right. That's hard to do," he said in mock admiration.

She paused in her fury for a moment. "I don't have any idea what that means." She frowned.

"I know you don't," he told her.

"But I know you were hired to lead a cattle drive not be a damn stud. Is that all you ever think about?"

"A nipple a day keeps the doctor away," he said affably.

"Bastard," she hissed. "I'm convinced now I was right all along. Haskell's not coming all this way after us. You looked us over, saw this might be a good-time chance. That's why you've taken this long way. You're just using it for the chance to enjoy yourself."

"You hang on to your wrong ideas, don't you?" he said mildly.

108

His calmness made her sputter rage. "Wrong? I'm not wrong. That's what you're doing, turning the drive into one big whoring time for yourself. I wonder who you've got lined up next," she shouted.

"You're jealousy is showing again." He grinned.

Her arm came up in a wild, furious swing which he blocked with ease. "Bastard," she hissed, stepped back as she saw his eyes harden. "I'd tell everyone about you but I don't want to get others in trouble."

"Now, that's the first smart thing you've said," Fargo agreed calmly.

She moved back to the bay, drew herself up in one swift motion. "Bastard," she flung back at him again and sent the bay storming down the hillside. Fargo drew a deep breath and returned to the bedroll, this time to sleep the rest of the night.

7

After he woke with the first dawn, he dressed and rode to the crest of the hill, his lake-blue eyes scanning the land ahead. Colorado Territory, fertile, green land, hills rising on both sides with heavy tree cover. Far ahead, too far to see yet, the great mountains rose to touch the sky. He turned the horse and went back down the hill to where Barney McCall had coffee ready, the others gathering around for the hot brew. Bart Dodd was sitting up in the wagon but he still looked like a man without blood inside him. As Fargo passed, Sandra's eyes met his in quiet, private exchange. Fargo dismounted, took the mug of coffee from Barney. Liz stood apart from the others, wearing a deep-red blouse that echoed the anger still in her high-planed, handsome face.

Fargo looked over the rim of the coffee mug at the others. The easy success of the drive this far could explode around them this day, or on the morrow, anytime, any moment. He had to find out as much as he could before it happened and he'd need someone to ride with him, someone he could send back if he were right. Slowly, he went over those gathered in front of him. Any of the Downer boys would do, as would Ed Norbert, Sewall, or Walsh. But he eliminated them. They'd be needed with the herd. They'd be the heart of moving the herd fast and hard if he sent word.

But they couldn't handle this large a herd alone. He'd keep Cassie and Carrie and Henrietta Baker with them. His eyes paused at Amanda Koster. The woman was big enough and strong enough but he'd watched her on horseback. She was a plodding rider, good enough to herd steers but not for what he'd need. His eyes continued on around the others. The Reverend was out of the question, Mrs. Downer and Sandra had their wagons to handle and he didn't know if Sophie could do much more than sit on a horse.

His gaze came to a halt again, on Bobby Dodd. The youngster was a good horsemen, sober, reliable beyond his years, but he was still only a twelve-year-old and Fargo's eyes moved to the last figure, Liz Ryan, still looking dark as she sipped her coffee. She was the only one who fitted and could be spared from the herd. She had the fire not to freeze up under pressure and, most important, she could ride fast. He straightened up, finished his coffee, and went over to her. She saw him approach, glared at him at once.

"You're riding with me today," he said curtly. "Get your horse."

Surprise mixed with protest flooded her face. "Why?" she asked.

110

"Because I'll want somebody with me and you're elected," he said.

"I think you'd more enjoy Cassie or Carrie," she said tartly.

"I would but I'm taking you. Now get moving," he snapped. He saw her consider refusing, decide against it, and he caught the flicker of curiosity that crept into her eyes before she strode away. He turned to where Ed Norbert and Walsh were emptying their coffee mugs.

"We're in Colorado Territory. I'm going on ahead. You keep the herd moving straight on. You're in charge of that, Norbert," Fargo said. "But I want everyone to stay in tight and be ready to move 'em where I say if I send word back."

"You really expecting trouble?" the man asked.

Fargo shrugged. "I don't know. I want to know about it before it happens, though. I don't like surprises." The man signified his understanding and Fargo climbed onto the pinto. "Remember, everyone stays in tight, including the wagons," he said.

"I got you," Norbert said, and Fargo spurred the pinto forward, waved to the twins as he left the campsite. Liz waited on the bay, fell alongside him, her face set tight, her lips a thin line. He was content to let her ride in angry silence. No arguments, no distractions, and he let his concentration focus on the task ahead. He rode along the grassy flat land between the thick timber stands, bur oaks and shagbark hickory, balsam and bitternut. He rode in a zigzag pattern, from one side to the other, his eyes scanning the near and the far, the ground underfoot, and the distant land. Liz rode along, slightly behind most of the time, following his erratic movements. She continued her disapproving, angry silence and he paid it no heed, busy with his own task.

They'd ridden perhaps a mile when he veered to

111

the right, drew up before the ravinelike stretch of land. Solid banks of trees lined both sides and he rode into the funnellike passage, followed it until it suddenly stopped, the trees on each side coming together to form a wall at one end. He turned, surveyed the green ravine. It was some twenty-five yards wide, maybe a hundred and fifty yards long. A box canyon with trees instead of rock, he murmured silently, permitted himself a moment of satisfaction.

He met Liz's eyes, saw the probing curiosity in them as she continued to stay silent, and he rode back out of the tree-lined box canyon. He crossed the flat land to the other side of the grassy plains where a low hill rose in a gentle incline. Liz followed and stayed just back of him as he slowed, moved along the edge of the flat grass, sweeping the ground with his eyes. He'd gone another mile or more when he heard Liz's voice, icy exasperation in it, as she broke her silence.

"Just what are we doing?" she snapped.

"Making plans. Looking," he said.

"For what?" she returned.

He halted, pointed to a brook that appeared and ran parallel to the grassy flat area. "That," he said, swung from the pinto, and squatted down beside the brook. She came to stand beside him and he gestured to the hoofmarks in the soft earth that bordered the brook. He moved, traced the line of hoofmarks, covering both sides of the brook. Too many, he grunted silently.

"Indians?" she asked.

"No. These horses have shoes, every one of them. About thirty, I make it," Fargo said grimly. "Haskell."

"Way up here ahead of us?" She frowned.

"Why not? He just rode on, giving us plenty of distance. He probably moved at night to make sure I wouldn't pick up any dust trails," Fargo said. He gestured to the ground again, where the tracks left the softness near the brook and pressed down the grass crossing the flat land. "They crossed over here and backtracked some."

"Where are they now?" she asked.

His eyes swept the thick woodlands that rose on both sides of the flat land. "Somewhere in there, on both sides, I'd guess. On ahead a ways, waiting," Fargo said.

"We go back and warn the others then," Liz said.

"You go back," Fargo said. "And you do more than warn them. You ride back and tell Ed Norbert to drive the herd into the box canyon we found. You can lead him to it."

He saw the frown dig into her forehead instantly. "Into the box canyon?" she echoed.

"The herd first, then the wagons," he said. "Close up the entrance with the wagons and take up positions behind them."

"That's crazy," Liz said. "Going into the box canyon is putting yourself in a trap."

"Yes, but that kind of trap is the best place to be now," Fargo said.

Her stare carried disagreement, suspicion, and the anger that was still inside her. "It's mad. Trapping ourselves is exactly what Haskell would like," she protested.

Fargo felt his temper soaring. "Dammit, you're wasting time and every minute counts. If they pass that box canyon they'll never have time to turn the herd back into it," he said.

Her frown stayed, deepened. "It's not right, trapping ourselves. Nothing about this whole drive has been right. This certainly isn't," she insisted.

"I do the thinking, not you, and there's no time to draw diagrams. Now get your ass in the saddle and

113

hightail it back to Norbert before it's too late," Fargo said.

She stared at him a moment more, whirled, climbed onto the bay and the frown of protest and uncertainty still dug into her brow. She cast another piercing glance at him and slapped the bay hard, sent the horse racing off. Fargo remounted, followed at a slower pace, reined up after a few hundred yards, and watched Liz until she was out of sight. He turned the pinto around, slowly moved to the line of trees at the bottom of the hillside at the left. Nobody had appeared to give chase after the girl but that didn't mean too much. Haskell could be watching and still playing his cards very carefully. Or he could have his men farther on, waiting to spring their ambush. Fargo rode into the edge of the trees, dismounted, and pulled the pinto inside the tree line where the cool darkness provided shelter and invisibility.

He sat down between two sturdy bur oaks with their deep-lined gray-brown bark. He had only to wait. When the herd failed to come along, Haskell would have to come out into the open. He'd have to move out to see what happened to his quarry. Fargo shifted against the tree. He'd stay hidden, watch Haskell lead his men out, move down to search along the flat, grassy land. He'd wait and watch, hang back, Fargo planned, until Haskell had moved down far enough to reach the box canyon. Haskell would have to attack, his plans frustrated. He'd lose heavily trying to storm his way into the box canyon but he'd have no choice but to try.

Fargo allowed himself a satisfied smile. He'd ride in from behind the attackers, then. He ought to be able to cut down at least six, a respectable number. If Haskell's force could be cut in half the man might well decide to go home and lick his wounds. If he decided to try again, he'd be much less a danger. Fargo let thoughts idle, stretched in the shade of the trees, lazily watched the sunlit, grassy flat land. Black-tailed jackrabbits with their oversize ears bounded back and forth across the grass. A pair of polecats marched serenely along the edge of the grass. A cluster of white-footed mice chased each other and he watched two does venture out into the sunlight only to leap back into the safety of the woodlands.

His eyes moved along the trees in the distance but there was no sign of Haskell's boys. They were staying well back, waiting, and Fargo smiled to himself. Within an hour they'd become concerned and move out to investigate. Fargo leaned his head back, let his eyes half-close as he listened to the forest sounds. It was perhaps fifteen minutes later when he heard the sound, not that of horse's hooves, not the sound of leather slapping against leather, the soft rattle of rein chains. He heard the low bellow of a steer, snapped his eyes open. Another low bellow drifted to him and then the soft rumbling sound along the ground. He felt a frown digging into his brow, sat up, swung onto one knee. Inside him, disbelief clung. He was imagining, sound playing tricks on him. Perhaps he'd dropped off to sleep, dreamed for a moment. He listened and the sound came again, multiplied this time, unmistakable. He felt his lips moving, words still inside them, and he stared down the flat land, disbelief still struggling to stay alive. A faint spiral of light dust rose into the air and the sounds became louder. The first of the steers came into sight in the distance, moving slowly along.

Fargo rose and the words whirling inside him found whispered breath. "Goddamn. What in the hell," he muttered. "Sonofabitch. The box canyon. Why the hell aren't they in the box canyon?" The question spun in his head, dangling in front of him. He stared at the herd as more of the steers came into view, his black brows pressed low, his mouth hanging open as disbelief tried to cling. They had disregarded his orders. *Why?* He almost shouted the question. Had something happened to Liz? His eyes swept the approaching herd. The wagons had been lined up across the rear of the herd, he saw. Billy Walsh rode at the left flank, Amanda Koster on the right. He saw Norbert and Sewall, rifles across their laps, riding beside the line of wagons, and then his glance halted as he found Liz on the bay, moving alongside the chuck wagon. She had made it back. Why the hell had Norbert disobeyed his orders?

Fargo saw that the others, Cassie and Carrie, Bobby Dodd, the Downer boys, and Henrietta Baker, had disappeared into the wagons. Norbert had been warned the attack might come and he'd taken defensive action. It made the question blaze even more furiously. Why hadn't he headed into the box canyon? *Shit*, Fargo muttered. He was watching a disaster about to happen. His eyes went to the wagons again. Norbert had lined them up so they could level a barrage of self-protective fire, the one supporting the other. Logic that was made of holes. They had no mobility and only defensive firepower. It didn't matter, really. Haskell wouldn't give a shit about them. He was probably laughing already.

The herd moved closer and Fargo's eyes moved to the heavy timber on the opposite hillside. He was watching as the horsemen burst out, split into two groups that peeled off to move independently. Thirty at least. He grimaced. He saw Fred Haskell's curly black hair as the man led one of the two groups. Blakelock Haskell rode with the other group, staying in with the main body of riders. Fargo watched and heard himself cursing softly, a wellspring of fury and frustration welling up inside him. The two groups split into four and he watched the men race at the herd, whirling and turning, yelling and waving lariats. The steers began to break up at once as the riders singled out small groups, drove them off.

Fargo heard the first crack of the rifle fire as those inside the wagons began to open up. Haskell's men paid little heed to the shots, bent low in the saddle, all but ignoring the fire as they raced back and forth, cutting the herd into fragments, chasing each small cluster along the flat land. Fargo watched one of Haskell's squads race along the edge of the herd, circle to gallop along behind the line of wagons. They poured a hail of gunfire into the wagons, not taking time to aim, their purpose to keep the others busy returning fire as the herd was decimated, run off in little clusters. Fargo took the heavy Sharps from the saddle holster, swung onto the pinto. It would be but an empty gesture, now, most of the herd already chased off in all directions, most already out of sight with one squad of Haskell's men concentrating on the pursuit. He moved from the shelter of the trees, sent the pinto racing along the edge of the tree line, the rifle at his shoulder. He fired twice and two of Haskell's men catapulted out of their saddles.

A second group had turned, joined the first in pouring fire into the wagons from a running line, Indian fashion. Fargo fired again, a tall man on a gray, watched the figure fall forward, drop over the horse's neck as the animal continued to run with its lifeless rider. The scene had become chaos, with some of Haskell's men still chasing off the last of the herd, others turning to join those pouring fire into the line of wagons which had come to a halt. Haskell had hired a rough lot of gunslingers, Fargo saw, fired again, and a fourth one toppled from his horse. He saw Fred Haskell on the far side, the man whirling his horse, gesturing in Fargo's direction, and a half-dozen riders started for him. Fargo whirled the pinto in a tight circle, staying low in the saddle as a hail of shots passed over his head. He bolted back into the tree line, leaped to the ground and whirled, on one knee, aiming at the riders rushing at him. He fired once, twice, and two of the men hit each other as they fell sideways from their horses.

The others reined up, spun their horses, suddenly unwilling to race into his fire. He took the few seconds to shove a new load of cartridges into the rifle, fired again and another of the men flew from his horse, hitting the ground as his chest spurted a stream of red. The other two ducked low and raced away. He saw one shudder, half-rise in the saddle, and topple to the ground. The shot had come from one of the wagons. Fred Haskell backed away, joined with another dozen of his men, and waved off the assault on the wagons. They rode away at full gallop and Fargo saw Blakelock Haskell in the distance, waiting with the rest of his men.

The sound of gunfire became but an echo and that drifted away to leave an eerie silence. Fargo moved from the trees, leading the pinto behind him. His glance swept the ground where he walked and then that around the wagons. He made a grim count. Ten of Haskell's men lay lifeless, seven he had brought down himself. Ten, he muttered, not nearly enough. Haskell still had at least twenty more, not that it mattered much now. The others were moving from the wagons and Fargo walked toward them. Sewall lay dead from multiple wounds, Walsh's form only a few feet from him. Fargo saw Barney McCall on the ground, Mrs. Downer wrapping a cloth around a wound in his left leg. He saw Sam Sturdivent's figure draped lifelessly over the tailgate of Amanda Koster's seed-bed wagon. His eyes moved to where the Downer boys were helping Sandra carry Bart Dodd out of the wagon. His need to prove himself was over.

Three shots had gone through his chest, Fargo saw, another through his neck. He'd probably been unable to move fast enough in the wagon. Sandra stood with her arms around the boy, his face pressed against her.

Fargo's eyes hardened as he saw Ed Norbert pulling himself into view from behind the Reverend's wagon, the man holding his shoulder which was soaked in red. The Reverend was murmuring a prayer at the edge of his wagon and just to his left, Liz, green eyes hollow, leaned against the bay. Fargo kept his hands at his sides, forced his fists to unclench as he strode toward Norbert.

"Why, goddamn you, why?" he flung at the man. "Why, didn't you go into the box canyon? Why'd you disobey my orders?" Ed Norbert stared at him. "The herd would've been safe there. That's all Haskell wanted, the herd, scatter them all over Colorado. He didn't give a shit about the rest of you."

"You didn't say anything about going into the box canyon," Ed Norbert said, wincing with pain as he spoke.

"The hell I didn't. I sent Liz back with that order," Fargo half-shouted. He saw Ed Norbert turn, look back at Liz, his eyes wide, his jaw hanging. Slowly, the man turned back to Fargo.

"She never told me," he said, shaking his head slowly. "She never said a damn thing about it."

Fargo's eyes slowly lifted, found Liz Ryan. He felt the consuming fury start to gather inside him, ballooning into a wild rage. He ran his tongue over his lips, found his voice as he stared at the girl. "You never told him," he said softly, each word coated with ice. "You never gave him my orders." He started to move toward her and his eyes were blue-fire shale. "Bitch," he almost whispered. "Goddamn bitch."

Liz Ryan's lips were parted and in her eyes he saw the pain, a terrible guilt stark in their green depths.

She watched him move toward her, saw the raging fury in him, and fear joined the guilt in her eyes. Her lips moved but no sound came, not even half-formed words. She seemed transfixed, her eyes staring at him with the pain and guilt and fear all swimming turbulently inside the forest green orbs. "Goddamn you," Fargo half-whispered as he continued toward her, his fists clenched. She blinked and an anguished sound tore from her. He was almost at her as she spun, leaped into the saddle, sent the bay into a full gallop at once. Fargo reached for her, missed and saw the bay go full out. The towering rage inside him exploding, he yanked the Colt from its holster, leveled it after the fleeing figure.

"*Fargo, no!*" he heard Barney McCall's anguished voice cry out.

He held Liz Ryan in his sights for a moment, his finger trembling against the trigger, and then he lowered the gun, dropped his arm to his side. He turned, met Barney McCall's eyes, and saw the gratitude there. "Thanks," the man murmured. "I'm beholden to you for that."

He pulled himself to his feet, leaned against the chuck wagon, and in his eyes he carried shared guilt and despair. "She didn't trust you, I guess," he said. "She must have thought you were setting us up."

"She'd no goddamn business deciding that," Fargo bit out.

Barney shrugged helplessly. "She knows now. She's seen now and there's only pain and guilt in her now. That's why she ran. I know her. She won't come back."

"Yes, she will," Fargo growled. "I'm going after her. Running, looking to get herself killed, that's too easy for her. She's going to live with this."

He saw the twins standing by the Reverend's wagon, their young, eager faces suddenly full of years. Mrs. Downer had moved to begin patching Ed Norbert's shoulder. Sophie had crawled from the seed-bed wagon after Sam Sturdivent had been lifted to the ground and now she clung to Amanda Koster's big form.

"What now?" Norbert asked. "What do we do if you're going chasin' after her?"

Fargo thought for a moment, heard Mrs. Downer's voice full of quiet resignation. "There's nothing to do but turn back," she said. "The herd's gone, scattered all over the land. We'll go back, gather our things before Haskell takes them with our lands."

"It's over," Norbert said softly. "Damn them all."

"We could go back and tell the sheriff. We'll all swear to what Haskell did here," Bess Sturdivent spoke up.

"Our word against the Haskells'," Jeff Downer answered. "They wouldn't believe us, not even if Fargo swore to it. We hired him, they'd say."

Fargo felt eyes turning to him. "I'm afraid Jeff's right on that. Haskell will swear you lost your herd on the trip and came back with this story to get him off your backs. He'll have his men back him up on it," the Trailsman said. "Maybe it's over, and maybe it's not," he added, drew a deep breath inward.

"How's that?" Barney asked.

"I can't say yet but I want to nose around some, after I catch hold of Liz Ryan," he said. "You do your burying here, that'll take most of what's left of the day. Move on and make camp someplace. In the morning, keep going due west, as if you were driving the herd."

"How long?" Norbert asked.

"Till I come to meet you," Fargo said, climbed back on the pinto.

"Fargo," Barney called to him. "What if you don't find her?"

121

"I'll find her," Fargo said grimly. He waved to the others, exchanged quick glances with Sandra Dodd as she watched him ride off with eyes full of sadness, the boy still beside her. The twins didn't smile as he passed and he sent the pinto into a fast trot, moved out of sight of the others in a few minutes. The grass was trampled by the herd and by Haskell's riders but Liz Ryan had been racing straight ahead. It was likely she'd stay headed that way, riding in a kind of mindless anguish. He moved on along the flat grass, saw where Haskell's riders had sent the small clusters of steers off to the sides, scattering them down little paths and up into the low hills. The grass began to grow straight, untrammeled, and the single line of Liz's horse became clear as a beacon.

She'd ridden the bay too hard and Fargo saw the horse's stride grow short, the trail along the new grass becoming uneven as the animal became too tired to run in a straight line. She had slowed, finally, he saw, walked the horse toward an area of trees and low hills bordered with rock formations. He followed, saw the marks leave the grass plains and climb into the hills. The bay was moving slowly, now, and as the hill grew steep he saw where Liz had slid from the saddle to walk on foot beside the horse. A stream came into view, running down along the succession of low hills, through wooded terrain. Fargo halted to examine the land on the other side of the stream. No hoofprints, he grunted silently. She had taken the horse up, walked through the stream to cool feet and ankles.

The day was closing down, Fargo noted, the gray deepening the wooded terrain quickly. He rode the pinto into the stream, pointed the horse up along the swift-running, cool water. As he moved on his eyes scanned both sides of the stream, watching the soft earth for signs of a footprint or a hoofmark. Darkness came to plunge the woods into pitch blackness and

Fargo turned the pinto out of the stream, dismounted, and found a place near the sound of the running water where the pinto had room to forage and he to lay out his bedroll. He'd have to wait till dawn. She could have turned out of the stream anywhere and he'd miss it in the inky blackness of the woods. He lay down, suddenly feeling bone-weary. Before he slept, the wild battle crept back in his mind and he saw the herd being scattered to the winds. His rage at Liz Ryan flooded back over him and he slept with it full inside him.

It was there when he woke with the dawn, washed in the cold waters of the stream, and moved on again. He rode alongside the stream, now, making faster time as once again he scanned both soft banks. She had followed the stream high into the hills, almost to a distant waterfall he saw, and then his eyes caught the hoofmarks moving along the bank, turning from the stream to go deeper into the woods. His practiced eye saw the tiny broken twigs where she had brushed past the thick trees. She seemed to move aimlessly, wandering through the terrain, and then he glimpsed the waterfall, close at hand. She had made a half-circle, come at the waterfall from the other side. He pulled the pinto to a halt as his ears, keen as a mountain lion's, caught the sound of a horse blowing air. He slid from the saddle, moved forward on foot. The horse snorted again, the sound alongside the waterfall. Fargo took the pinto halfway, draped the reins over a low branch, and moved forward.

On silent feet, he climbed over flat rock and the sound of the waterfall was loud now, splashing water and sounds of spray bouncing up. A tiny cloud of spray mist rose from the site and he pushed his way through the coarse-toothed leaves of a box elder. The waterfall came into sight, and, on the flat rocks beside it, her figure, knees drawn up, head buried into her hands. She looked pitiful, despondent, and he felt the rage soar inside him. She'd no right to look pitiful, damn her. He stepped into the open and she heard him, lifted her head, met his icy stare. He saw the fright come into her eyes, stay for but a moment, and then give way to something else, part defeat and part defiance, part guilt and part anger.

"What do you want here?" she cast out as she rose to her feet.

"You're going back," he said.

"No, never," she threw back.

"Yes," he growled. "Running's too easy. You're not taking that way out."

"Leave me alone," she shouted.

"No way," he said implacably.

"I can't undo it," she said with a burst of anguish. "God, I wish that I could. I was wrong, all wrong. I know that now."

"Not just wrong. That makes it sound like an honest mistake," he flung back at her.

Her eyes grew wary. "That's what it was," she said.

"Hell it was. You didn't trust me because of Blanche Haskell and the others. It was that damn jealousy sticking in you and your wrong-headed arrogance and that's no honest mistake," he returned. "That's pure, rotten bitchiness and a lot of dreams are dead because of it and a lot of people, and by Christ you're not just going to run away from it."

She started to turn to flee but his arms shot out, caught hold of her. "Let me go, damn you," she shouted, kicked at his groin. He twisted, took the blow on the hard muscle of his thigh. He spun her around, flipped her over, and she fell onto her back. She tried kicking him again as he sidestepped, got a hand at the top of her trousers, yanked, and the buttons flew open. "No, damn you," she screamed, clawed at his face. He put his head down low and her nails caught at his hair, pulled, and he winced as he yanked hard at the trousers. They came down, past her knees, lithe, lovely legs kicking free. He rolled her on her stomach as she screamed and swore as a pert rear pushed up tight pink bloomers edged with lace. His hand reached out as she tried to scoot forward, seized the waist of the bloomers, and tore them back. Her white, twin little mounds rose up and she screamed. "Goddamn you, I'll kill you," she swore, tried to pull her legs up.

He grabbed her ankles, flipped her over and pulled the bloomers from her. She twisted away, turned her rear to him, and tried again to scoot forward. His hand came down hard and the sharp sound bounced from the rocks. She screamed and he got one arm around her waist, pulled her back, rolled her over his knees as her legs kicked wildly. He began to slam his hand down on the white, wriggling rear, but no spanking slaps, each one a tremendous blow that had her rear burning red in moments. Her curses became screams and the screams turned to shuddering wails as he beat her rear until it was nothing but red.

He stopped, stood up, yanking her with him. Swinging her into his arms, he flung her into the cold pool at the base of the waterfall. The cries turned to sharp screams and he watched her go under, come up spitting out water, dog-paddle away from him to rest against the far side of the little pool. She rested there, her red shirt soaked, outlining the sharp points of her upturned breasts, and she gulped in big draughts of air, her eyes blazing fury at him. The cold water was quickly taking the stinging pain from her rear, he knew, and he let her stay in a few minutes longer, then started around the edge of the rocks toward her. She pushed herself away but he flung off shirt, boots, and trousers, stepped in after her. She swung at him, sending spray high in the air as he reached for her.

He caught her hair as she tried to dive away, yanked her back and she cried out.

"Let me go, goddamn you," she screamed at him as he dragged her from the water, flung her onto the grass that edged the rock around the pool. She bounced, her legs flying into the air for a second, coming down at once, and he glimpsed the smooth tan belly and the wide, luxuriously thick dark triangle. He pulled her back as she drew her knees up again, turned away from him, and his hand pulled the buttons open on the red blouse. "What are you doing?" she flung at him, the green eyes wide.

"I'm going to collect on that race," he said.

Her hands tried to claw at him but he knocked them aside and yanked the blouse from her. She fell back onto the grass, the smallish breasts not as small as they'd always seemed but as deliciously peaked, full undersides that turned up to sharp, pink-brown nipples, each surrounded by a brown circle. He dropped half-over her, closed one hand over each breast. "No, I won't, no, damn you," she gasped at him. "I won't let you. I don't want you."

"That's the last of your lies," he said, pressed his mouth on hers, forced her lips apart, and sent his tongue probing hard, circling, demanding.

"No," she managed to murmur, the sound made of breathy protest. His mouth stayed on hers and he felt her lips lose their hardness, grow soft, close around his. "No," she breathed again and this time there was more breath than protest. He took his mouth from hers, pressed it over her left breast, and felt the shudder go through her. Her fists pounded against his shoulder blades. "No, goddamn you, Fargo, no. No, you bastard, no," he heard her saying as the pink-brown nipples grew hard under his kisses, rising in his mouth. He sucked on her breast, gently, letting his tongue circle the edges of the pink-brown areolas.

126

"Oooooh . . . oh, damn you," she gasped. Her fists against his shoulder blades opened, fingers clutching at him. He took his mouth from her breast and she instantly began to struggle again. The anger still in him, he pressed his leg between her thighs, forced her legs open. "No, dammit . . ." she started to cry out as his mouth seized her breast again, took almost all of the piquant upturned little mound in. "Aaaaah . . . oh, God," she breathed.

He pulled himself atop her, felt his maleness pushing, swollen hard, an ageless echo of anger and desire, one becoming the other, emotions mingling together until there was only the terrible wanting and reasons were no longer important. He touched her soft entrance with his tip. Again she cried out refusal, murmured protest, and for an instant he wondered, then thrust into her and felt the smile form inside him. The body gives the lie to words, unwilling to play the deceits of the mind. She was wet, wonderfully wet and lubricious, the wanting no words could deny. He moved quickly in her, harshly, the very harshness its own wild ecstasy, and suddenly her arms were around him, her abdomen sucking in and out as she responded to his every thrust. The saucy breasts rose up for him, nipples hardened, and he felt her hands moving up and down his back. He continued to thrust roughly and her gasps were matching his motions.

"Fargo . . . Fargo," she said, her voice a whisper now. He felt her abdomen begin to quiver, outer muscles first, then inner ones. Her long legs clasped hard around him, strained to hold him deep inside her. "Oh, oh, Jesus . . . aaaaggghh," she cried, her cry a hoarse sound, and she quivered violently in his arms as he let himself erupt with her. The quivering continued, only moments, yet it seemed as though she would never stop. But she fell away, drawing in gasps of air as she lay flat against the grass. He looked down at the loveliness of her slender, lithe form, the saucy high-pointed breasts, the narrow hips, and the thick luxury of her triangle. The body echoed the face, handsome, angular, full of spirit.

Her eyes opened, looked up at him, the brown flecks seeming larger. "I should hate you," she whispered.

"Not for that. You wanted that. You've wanted it all along," he said. "I didn't force you. I just tore the mask away."

She sat up as he rolled over to lay beside her, his eyes following the lovely contours of her body. She moved on her side and winced. "I can't sit, damn you," she said, her eyes glowering at him. His eyes gave her no sympathy. "Why did you do it?" she asked.

"Which?"

"Both. Fan my ass so hard I can't sit without hurting and then make love to me," she said.

He thought for a moment. "All part of the same thing, I guess. Anger, and wanting to take away all your hiding places."

She looked away. "I can't go back," she murmured.

"You're going back," he growled.

"I ran because I didn't care what happened to me. I hoped I'd meet a Kiowa or a Pawnee," she told him.

"Suicide. All your guilt paid off in one burst of self-sacrifice. The coward's way."

"I'm not a coward," she burst out angrily.

"Then get dressed and get your ass in that saddle, no matter how much it hurts," he said.

He saw her eyes turn soft moss-green as she stared at him. "Not until you make love to me again. I need that, not just for the pleasure. It's a strengthening, a reminding that those masks are gone and only the truth is left." She paused, watching his face. "But then you knew that all along, didn't you?" she finished.

"All along," He nodded as she leaned over to him, pressed herself against him, and pushed him down on the grass. The tiny points of the upturned breasts were still firm, pressing into his chest. Her legs moved and she rubbed the black, busy triangle across his groin. "No masks, damn you," she whispered, her mouth opening on his. She meant it, proved it as the bubbling sounds of the waterfall became a backdrop for her cries of pleasure and the morning became a private world.

Finally she slept in the hollow of his arm, on her side, until he stirred, woke her gently. She looked up at him and saw the sternness lining his face. "Get dressed," he said. "It's time to go back."

She rose, silent, put on her clothes dried in the heat of the sun, her face grave. He saw her wince as she climbed into the saddle. He walked to where he'd left the pinto, mounted the horse, and she swung in beside him. He saw her draw a deep breath, lift her chin high, as she rode off with him.

8

They'd ridden for most of the morning when, in the distance across the grassy plain, she saw the wagons moving slowly toward them. She came to a halt and he looked at her sharply, her lips parted, her fists knotting the reins together. "I can't," she breathed. "I can't face them."

"You can and you will," Fargo said firmly.

"What can I say to them? Words won't mean anything. Apologies are empty gestures, even if they believe me," she said and he heard the panic coming into her voice. "I can't do it. I can't face them," she repeated. She started to wheel the bay around and his hand shot out, caught hold of the reins and pulled the horse back around against the pinto. He shifted his grip from the reins to her hair, yanking her head back hard.

"*OWOOOO!*" She gasped.

"You'll face them, dammit. You're not running," he bit out angrily, released his hold on her hair. She leaned sideways, clutched at him, pressed herself against him across the two horses.

"Hold me, Fargo, please hold me, for a minute more," she whispered, almost a whimper. His arms gathered her in, one hand cupping the nearest upturned little breast, and he heard the long sigh that spiraled up from inside her. She clung to him for a long moment, finally drew away. "All right," she murmured gravely. "Let's go."

He moved forward slowly, her leg almost brushing his. She rode with chin up, her handsome face tight. The wagons came closer and he could see the Reverend's pared-down Conestoga leading the way. He heard Liz's voice, almost too low to catch. "What'll they do to me, Fargo?" she asked.

"They won't drag you behind the wagons. They're not that kind," he said. "Whatever they do, you'll live with it."

"I've nothing to tell them, no way to make it up to them," she said dully.

"Nobody expects speeches. You've come back. That'll say something of itself," he said. He moved the pinto into a trot and she followed at once. They reached the wagons a few minutes later and Fargo halted, saw Ed Norbert on his horse, riding with his shoulder bandaged. Cassie and Carrie rode together, alongside Sandra Dodd's wagon, and Fargo saw Sandra's round, deep eyes meet his quick glance. Another kind of acceptance laced their depths now. Bobby Dodd rode beside the Downer boys and Amanda Koster sat in her wagon with Sophie, her horse hitched behind. Harry and Bess Sturdivent rode together and Fargo watched as eyes turned to Liz. No one spoke, their eyes and faces more eloquent than any words. He watched Liz meet each harsh, burning stare, no defiance in her answering glance, just acknowledgment. She took their accusations with her own silence, no begging of the spirit, and he gave her credit for that. The anguish and the pain were searing inside her, he knew.

Barney McCall came down from his wagon, limping, his face drawn and tired. He reached up, took the reins of the bay, and tied them onto the side of the wagon, guiding the horse and Liz alongside the driver's seat. Again, words were unnecessary, no forgiveness in his gesture, only a silent sadness. As Fargo watched, he saw the others turn their faces away and give their answer. Liz saw it, too, sat silently but her slender body straight, only her eyes looking down at the reins of her horse. They would shun her, ignore and ostracize her, fling the silence of bitterness around her. It could corrode, shrivel, spear far more deeply than mere anger, each silent moment a soundless scream of accusation.

He turned away, too, guided the pinto to the front of the little ground, his eyes going to Ed Norbert first. "You can ride. Can you shoot?" he asked.

The man nodded. "If I have to," he said.

Fargo scanned the group with a quick glance. "I'm going back out to scout them. You just keep moving on," he told them.

"Why? There's no point in going on," Mrs. Downer said.

Fargo shrugged. "I'll answer that when I get back," he said.

"Whatever you say, Fargo," Ed Norbert cut in. "You've been on target so far. I'll go along with whatever you say."

A murmur of agreement rose and Fargo nodded, let his eyes linger on Liz for a moment. She lifted her head, gazed back with the green eyes so dark with pain they were almost black. He turned, swept the twins in a glance, Sandra and the others, cantered off, and headed along the center line of the grassy plain area. He cut sharply to the left in a few moments, moved from the flat land into the wooded hilly terrain, doubled back along the high ground, finally descending to the land below. He halted, his eyes sweeping the ground. The marks were all over, steers racing wildly to freedom, the rangehands pursuing them. Some swung off on their own tangents and he noted that each fragmented group ran with riders pursuing them.

Eyes narrowed, he began to move along the hill terrain, watching the tracks criss-cross, fan out, others returning, hoofprints clearly visible. He took note of numbers and direction and continued on as the day wore to a close. The land had narrowed, become an erratic funnel bordered by rolling hills. He halted, dismounted, ran his fingers over the trampled grass, studying the marks which, to his eyes, were a silent book, meanings and messages in every hoofprint and every line.

He swung back onto the pinto, the coldness of his eyes contrasting with the tiny smile that touched the corners of his mouth. The signs were beginning to form a pattern even as the night descended to blanket the land with blackness. He halted, rested, let the pinto graze, and waited for the almost full moon to start to ascend. As it began to cast its silver-gray light over the land, he rode on, slowly, carefully. He had taken a measure of a man's character and the trail signs were beginning to back his guess. The proof didn't lay far ahead, he was certain, and he steered the pinto higher on the hill land, moved silently through trees. He rose over a jog in the hills when his nostrils caught the scent of woodsmoke and he increased pace a fraction, continued to climb until he reined up abruptly. Below, in a long, large hollow, he saw the dull glow of the campfire, the figures spread out around it. Beyond them, his eyes took in the unshapen, mass of blackness and he heard the lowing of the bull-calves. His eyes picked out two riders slowly circling the herd to keep them calm.

Fargo let his eyes move back and forth across the dark mass that was the herd. All of it there, or damn near all of it. He slid from the saddle, lowered himself to the ground, and tied the pinto to a low branch well back of the edge of trees. He lay back, managed to sleep some to the familiar lowing of the steers. Dawn woke him instantly and he sat up, stayed behind the trees, and watched Haskell's men start to gather themselves. They moved casually, not even a single guard posted, the confidence of the victors. Fargo picked out Fred Haskell having coffee, saw the gray mane of Blakelock Haskell come into view, pause beside the young man, slap him on the arm.

Fargo stayed motionless, waited, his eyes scanning the scene. He wanted to see but one thing more now and he had to wait but a few minutes more when the men began to saddle up. He watched as they took to their mounts, began to move the steers. Slowly, they started to drive the herd, not back to the Texas Trail but due south toward New Mexico. Fargo rose, swung onto the pinto, and his eyes were made of blue quartz. He had the answer he had waited to find, wondered about, wanted to reject, and could only wait to see for himself. He began to ride back the way he had come, no need for hurrying. Haskell wouldn't push the herd now. There was no need and Fargo grunted grimly as he made the silent promise to himself.

It was late in the afternoon, the shadows growing long, when he returned to the wide grass plains and found the little cluster of wagons and the few riders looking pitifully lost. They halted as they saw the gleaming black-and-white horse riding toward them. Fargo swung from the saddle as he reached them, saw Liz riding apart from the others, at the rear of the chuck wagon. Barney McCall lowered himself to the ground, moved to the tail of the wagon.

"Coffee?" he asked. "The pot's still hot. We stopped for some only a little while ago."

"Yes," Fargo said, waited as the man brought him a mug, sipped it slowly, and felt the goodness of it going through him. The others had gathered around, eyes on him, Liz watching from the back of the semicircle. "You want to get your steers back?" he asked, saw the frowns come over their faces.

"It'd take months, if we could find them," Harry Sturdivent said.

"They're pretty much all in one place," Fargo said. "I had a hunch and I was right. Blakelock Haskell's a greedy man and once a greedy man always a greedy man. He couldn't let a good, salable herd just run off and go to waste. He had his boys round them up, or most of them, anyway. All we have to do is take them back."

He heard Ed Norbert's snort. "That's all, eh?" the man said.

Fargo nodded, said nothing.

"Could we do it?" Jim Downer spoke up. "I mean, do we have a chance?"

"A chance," Fargo answered. "A chance to get

134

yourselves killed, too." His glance traveled over the ground. He put aside Sophie and the Reverend at once, added Mrs. Downer. That left fourteen able to ride and shoot. Of those fourteen, how many could shoot fast and straight, he pondered. Barney McCall, Amanda Koster, Liz, the three Downer boys, Harry Sturdivent, Bobby and Ed Norbert. Henrietta Baker, he added. She could probably shoot with the best of them. Ten in all, and himself.

"You're counting chances," he heard Ed Norbert say and he nodded. "I figure maybe ten who can ride and shoot," the man said.

"That's what I figure," Fargo agreed.

"Haskell's got to have twenty or more hands left," Norbert said. "All gunslingers. Too much, too many," he bit out.

"The odds are what you make out of them," Fargo said. "Every gambler will tell you that. Buck them and you're a sure loser. Use them and you can win."

"How do you figure to cut them?" the man asked.

"Haskell's riding high. He figures you're all headed back. He's not expecting any kind of trouble," Fargo said. "This time we'll do the surprising." He let his eyes sweep the others, saw thoughts turning behind each face.

"Why not?" Harry Sturdivent said. "We've damn little left to live for anyway. Might as well give it a last try."

"I've lived a long time already," Henrietta Baker said. "Besides, I want my steers back."

"I've never liked going back to nothing," Amanda Koster growled.

"Then it's settled," Fargo said. "We'll need the extra horses. Unhitch all but three wagons. We'll take Sandra's big rack bed, Mrs. Downer's converted farm dray, and the chuck wagon. Sophie and the Reverend will stay with the wagons, along with Mrs. Downer. The rest of you will use the extra horses."

"What's your plan?" Norbert asked.

"I'll tell on on the way. Meanwhile, get those wagons unhitched and your personal gear on the horses," Fargo ordered. He watched as wagons were pushed to one side, unhitched, horses saddled, and his orders put into effect. There were but a few hours of daylight left when they were ready to head out again, a reformed group. Mrs. Downer drove her wagon and the Reverend held the reins of Sandra Dodd's heavy rack bed. Barney brought up last with the chuck wagon.

Sandra and the twins rode up to flank Fargo as he surveyed them once more, Ed Norbert at his side. "We'll just make time for now. I figure we'll catch up to them after dark tomorrow night. They'll just be about crossing into New Mexico then. You'll all get your orders then but I'll tell you this much now. We're going to have to hit hard and with surprise. That's the only way we'll have any chance. You'll all use your rifles. You'll all do exactly what you're assigned to do or it'll go sour. Now let's move," Fargo said.

"One thing, Fargo," he heard Harry Sturdivent call out, saw the man's eyes go to Liz. The others followed his gaze. "She stays out of it," the man said. "We do it ourselves."

"We need every one we have, every gun, every rider," Fargo said.

"Not her," the man said. "It's our lives, all or nothing, and that's because of her. We don't want her kind of help."

Fargo scanned the others, their silence his answer. He was asking everything else of them. He'd no right to demand more. Emotions didn't back down to logic. He looked at Liz, her face in shadow as she gazed down at her hands, but he could see the tight line of her jaw. He shrugged. "Move out," he said quietly, sent the pinto on to take the lead.

It was after they made camp that Cassie and Carrie came to sit beside him, their bright faces clouded. "We're sorry about Liz," the one said.

"But we can't say Harry Sturdivent's wrong," the other added.

"Wrong, right, maybe none of it matters a tinker's damn. It's what you feel inside that counts," Fargo said. "Or maybe some things are right and wrong all at the same time."

They thought for a moment, identical frowns furrowed exactly the same in their identical brows. Together, they leaned forward, kissed his cheeks lightly. "Maybe," they whispered in unison, hurried off together. Fargo spread his bedroll, undressed, and slept quickly. The final time would come soon enough.

He had them off to an early start in the morning sun and held back not to lose sight of the wagons that had slow going up the hills. At one point he rode back to help pull the heavy rack-bed rig, noticing the Reverend, unused to the wagon, in trouble. He waited as Barney got the chuck wagon over the bad spots, came alongside Liz. Her eyes met his, the pain in them veiled.

"Sorry," he said. She'd know what he meant.

"You tried," she answered, her voice dull, flat.

"Just hang in," he said.

She made a harsh sound. "Every night I want to run again. I can feel their hate all around me. I don't know how much more I can take."

"The hate they have for you?" he questioned. "Or the hate you have for yourself?"

"Does it matter?" she asked bitterly.

"It matters," he said and rode on to draw up alongside Ed Norbert. "We're making good time. We'll be close by dark," he said. "We're moving near New Mexico. The land's taking on a different face."

The man nodded, followed Fargo's eyes as the Trailsman took note of the drier soil, the scattered appearance of Joshua trees and manzanita bushes. When night came, a full moon arched across the sky. Fargo had them make camp but build no fire. He gathered them together, except for Liz, who stayed beside the chuck wagon.

"The Reverend, Mrs. Downer, and Sophie will stay here with the wagons," he began. "The rest of you will come with me, on foot, leading your horses. I figure Haskell's men aren't more than two or three ridges ahead. When we reach them, we're going to split up into three groups. We'll be higher than Haskell's outfit, looking down on them. Henrietta, Amanda, Barney, Harry Sturdivent will go with me. Jeff, Jim and Jack, Bess Sturdivent, Sandra, you'll go with Ed Norbert." He surveyed them, saw them nod in understanding, turned his glance to Carrie, Cassie, and Bobby Dodd. "You three are going to wait till the shooting starts, then, circling, you move down to ride herd on the steers. Stay low in the saddle and make for the front of the herd. You stay with the herd while we do the rest. Keeping the herd from bolting is your job. Everybody understand?"

They nodded and Fargo rose, took the pinto by the reins, and started walking, glanced back to see the others following in pairs. Liz remained behind the wagons, he saw. He continued on, carefully topping the first ridge of the hills, then the second. He was approaching the third when his ears caught the low bellow of the steer and he held one hand up for caution and silence. He moved forward on the balls of his feet, reaching the crest of the last ridge and motioning for the others to come up beside him. Below, the campsite was still, sleeping figures dotting the ground under the light of the full moon. The herd was a dark mass beyond the sleepers and his eyes spied the two riders slowly circling the steers. Another hour or so till dawn, he guessed by the position of the moon. His voice, whispered, nonetheless carried clearly along the top of the ridge.

"When the light comes, pick out your targets, a first one and then a second. Draw a bead and hold it. Fire when I do. If anybody's bothered by shooting a man having a cup of coffee they can leave now," Fargo said.

"Won't bother me any," Henrietta Baker answered. "They'd do it to me if they got the chance."

"All right, if you all shoot straight, I figure we'll cut the odds down by anywhere from eleven to fifteen with the first round," Fargo said. He glanced at Norbert. "Get over there on the right side of them," he said and watched as the man moved in a crouch, the three Downer boys following on his heels, Bess Sturdivent and Sandra drawing up at the rear, each carrying a rifle.

Fargo had taken the heavy Sharps from its saddle holster, moved to the left side of the ridge, Henrietta Baker following him, the others coming after her. He lay down atop the ridge after moving the pinto and the other horses behind the ridgeline out of sight. He drew a deep breath, let the time go by, and watched the moon moving out of sight. The first pink line appeared on the distant horizon, spreading with surprising speed, dawn hurrying itself over the hills. Fargo rested the rifle stock against his face, moving his eyes along the polished barrel. He drew a bead on a figure in a poncho, shifted the sights to a second man a few feet away.

The camp began to wake, men stretching, getting to their feet. He glimpsed Fred Haskell heading for another man heating coffee in a big enamel pot over a small fire. Fargo returned his sights to the man in the poncho. The figure moved, started to take off the garment. Fargo fired and the figure stiffened, headless inside the poncho, collapsed on the ground, its shroud in place. Both sides of the ridge exploded in gunfire and Fargo saw one of Haskell's men, coffee raised to his lips, pitch forward into the tin cup as he went down. Suddenly the camp seemed almost a ballet of twisting, falling figures as the cross-fire poured down with deadly effect and more accuracy than he'd hoped for. He spun, darted the few feet below the ridge line, and vaulted onto the pinto. "Let's go," he yelled and saw the others run for their horses.

Henrietta Baker was first behind him as he sent the pinto racing down the hillside. Below, Haskell's remaining men were running for their horses or diving for the cover of the nearest trees. Fargo saw Fred Haskell swing onto his horse, gun in hand, look up with astonishment still on his cruel-lipped face. He saw the riders coming down from both ridges, reined up to take aim. Fargo fired the Sharps as the pinto reached the bottom of the hill. He saw Fred Haskell's hat blow from his head and the man topple out of the saddle. Fargo raced the pinto directly at him, reached him just as Haskell regained his feet, brought his six-gun up to fire. The shot whistled past the Trailsman's head as he ducked to one side and Haskell tried to get off another shot, saw there was no chance, and dived away. The pinto's chest caught his legs as he leaped, sent him tumbling in a half-somersault. Fargo, turning in the saddle, the rifle at his shoulder, fired again. Fred Haskell's half-somersault took on one more turn and his form tumbled head-over-heels to lay on the ground, twitching, his black, curly hair turning a dark red.

Fargo, hunkered low in the saddle, saw the streaking shapes of Bobby, Cassie, and Carrie in the distance, racing along the front edge of the herd. Some of Haskell's men tried to pull together and he saw Ed Norbert, Amanda Koster, and the Downer boys cut them down with a concentrated hail of gunfire. He let his eyes sweep the scene. Four of the gunslingers were racing into the hills, not bothering to return fire. His eyes sought the gray-white mane of Blakelock Haskell among the still figures on the ground. It wasn't there. He reined up, let the pinto regain breath. The shouts and gunfire died away and a silence came over the scene. Fargo dismounted as the others came toward him, only Harry Sturdivent holding his arm.

"Nothing much," the man said. "Took a slug but it went through clean."

"We did it," Ed Norbert said. "Goddamn, we did it."

"They're finished," Amanda Koster said. "Cut up and done in."

Fargo saw Henrietta Baker watching him, waiting for his answer. "Probably," he agreed. "But we'll post sentry duty every night till we reach Socorra, just in case." He had just finished the sentence when the cry came out of the thick bank of trees near the ridge, Blakelock Haskell's voice, the roar of a wounded lion.

"Fargo, I want to get my son," the man called out. "No shooting. Just let me come down and get him."

"We're moving out soon. You can get him afterward," Fargo called back, hearing his voice echo in the hollow.

"I'll kill you for this, Fargo," the voice roared back from the trees. "With my bare hands I'll kill you one day."

"Go home, Haskell. It's over here," Fargo shouted. "Go home. You'll get your chance."

He waited but there was no answering shout and he nodded to Sandra and Harry Sturdivent. "Go back, get the others with the wagons and catch up to us," he said. They nodded, wheeled their horses around, and rode off at once. "We're moving on," Fargo told the others. "Start riding herd."

"Damn, that sounds mighty fine." Ed Norbert grinned. Fargo's eyes scanned the tree cover of the hills as they started to move forward. Haskell had perhaps only three or four men left with him. He'd not try anything now. Perhaps not at all. He'd been beaten soundly. They'd have at least a day, maybe two, to finish their burying. Fargo's lips turned down in bitterness. Rotten, all of it, the fruits of greed. He cast another glance at the trees as the herd began to go forward, rode on ahead, and by midday the wagons had caught up to them. Henrietta Baker rode beside him, her eyes bright as new tenpenny nails.

"You've done well by us, Fargo," the old woman said. "You think we're going to make it now?"

"Maybe," Fargo said.

"That's a hiding-place word. What're you thinking?"

"Anything can happen on a drive. Steers have been known to just give out. This herd didn't start out with a lot of extra strength. Then, this country's full of *banditos* who'd like a herd to drive to market."

"There's something more," the woman said, picking up the unsaid in his tone.

"It's called Apache," Fargo told her.

Henrietta nodded. "You see any signs?" she asked.

"Not yet," he answered. "That doesn't mean much. Not with the Apache."

"Thanks for being honest," the woman said as she rode after a straying steer. Fargo pushed on till night, posted the sentries in shifts. Precautions only. He'd all but written off Haskell for now. The man's fight was reduced to a personal vow now and he wouldn't get his few remaining hired hands to risk their necks on that score. He'd be needing to offer them a fat bonus

142

for that and he couldn't come through there, either. Fargo's eyes narrowed as he made the conclusion. He bedded down at the edge of the herd and slept soundly till the morning arrived.

He had the herd off to an early start and they moved deeper into New Mexico and the land became a different land of dry, sun-baked soil, fescue grass, ocotillo shrubs, chuperosa and mesquite. They moved through land where rock formations rose up on all sides, fell away only to appear again, the earth wearing its oldest face traversed by lines made of canyons and passages.

Fargo moved back and forth along the line of the herd, pausing to ride with first one, then the other of his remaining hands. Cassie and Carrie had regained most of their bubbliness and Sandra Dodd's eyes carried another kind of acceptance along with the hint of hope. He paused to ride with Liz, a lone figure pulling up at the back of the line, her chin held high but her eyes revealing the bitter pain inside her. "It'll be over soon," he told her.

"Not for me," she answered.

"You can't carry it around forever," he said sternly. "It's done with."

"No, not just like that," she said. "It never is." Her eyes found his. "You're the only good thing to come out of this for me, Fargo. You and your making me know myself."

"There'll be more out of it," he told her and rode on. Later that night, when the rest of the camp slept, he found her standing alone, watching the star-swept sky. "Stop eating yourself sick. That won't help. The others will come around. They need time," he said.

She shook her head. "Time's not enough. They need reason and there isn't any," she said. A wry smile edged her lips. "No more masks, remember?" she said.

"They'll come around," he repeated.

"No, besides, would it bring back those who died? Would it change the truth?" she said. "It wouldn't change what I did, or how I feel about it." She leaned her face on his chest for a moment, then pulled back. "Get away. No point in anyone seeing you being nice to me." She strode away and he let her go. He hadn't the words to help.

He had the herd moving again soon after dawn and he rode point, keeping a good distance ahead of them. The land narrowed and widened and narrowed again with the rock formations on both sides. The land was quiet, too quiet, and he felt himself growing nervous. The nervousness became more pronounced when he spotted the single tracks of a lone Indian pony. "Scout," he muttered grimly. He rode on but saw no other trails. The following morning he spied part of a moccasin, beadwork around the toe end, the angular pattern of the Apache designs. He found no other trail marks and his lips drew back in a grimace. A bad sign, not a good one. They were taking pains to erase their trail.

By nightfall he found a stream which ran through a stand of yucca and he ordered a halt, gathered the others around. "Move the wagons into the center of the herd," he said. "You'll sleep inside and underneath them," he said.

"You see signs?" Norbert questioned.

"Some," he admitted. "But that doesn't matter. This is Apache country. Being careful is staying alive."

He helped get the wagons inside the herd and the steers didn't crown them, willing to stay away. Fargo took bedroll, pushed through the herd, and made his way to a cluster of rocks some twenty-five yards from the camp. He lay down in the center of the rocks in a roomy-enough little area. He'd just taken his shirt off when he heard the voice, a whispered call. "Fargo . . ."

144

He saw the figure appear through the little crevice between the rocks, blond braids hanging over her breasts, one hand smoothing down the white peasant blouse. "What the hell are you doing here?" he barked.

Sophie offered a smile. "I wanted to come to see you," she said with a hint of coyness. Fargo started to shake his head, stopped as his eyes caught the movement at the crevice in the rocks, and Amanda Koster's big figure pushed its way into the little circle. Her face glowered and angry eyes focused on Sophie.

"Figured this is where you were heading," the woman growled. "What'd I tell you, dammit?"

Sophie's face fell into a sullen pout. "I wanted to come see him," she said.

"Shit you did. You want to see what he'd be like," the woman snarled. Her hand darted out, seized one blond braid, yanked forward with such force the girl fell to her knees as she yelped in pain. "Goddamn ungrateful little bitch," the big woman said. She backhanded Sophie across the face and the girl cried out.

"That'll be enough of that," Fargo said, stepping forward.

"Butt out, Fargo," Amanda Koster hissed, turning to him, and he saw the fury in her eyes. "You're not enjoying yourself with this little piece. She's mine, goddammit."

All the suspicions he had pushed aside came back, no longer any way to look away from them. But he didn't want trouble with the woman. She had pulled her weight and she was still needed. Her private life was her own problem and he wanted no part of it. "I was just going to send her back," he said.

Amanda Koster's eyes bored into him, her frown staying as she turned his words in her mind. "Maybe you were. She's been doin' all the chasin'-after, I know that," the woman said. "And after all I've done for her. I took her in, gave her board and food, a place to work."

The words were all surface talk. He knew that now with no more questions. The real reasons lay in their own darknesses. Take her back. Get some sleep. You may need it tomorrow," he said. The woman yanked hard on the blond braid, lifted Sophie to her feet, and the girl cried out in pain again. "No more rough stuff," Fargo said. "Leave her be." He met the woman's glower and let her see the ice in his eyes.

Amanda Koster nodded curtly, took her big hand from around Sophie's hair. "Come on," she snapped at the girl and Fargo saw Sophie fall in behind her, head lowered, her face sullen. He let his breath out in a deep sigh as they disappeared through the crevice, finished undressing, laid the Sharps beside him, and went to sleep. He slept fitfully, waking to listen to the night every half-hour, but the soft lowing of the steers was the only sound. He slept soundly before the morning came, woke refreshed enough, and led the herd forward as quickly as possible. He left Norbert to guide them and rode on but not before his eyes sought out Amanda Koster. She was in the wagon with Sophie and the girl had her arm linked into the big woman's grip, her head leaning on Amanda Koster's shoulder.

Everyone to their own thing, Fargo grunted silently, so long as they didn't bother him with it. He rode on out of sight of the herd. The rocks rose on each side of the arroyolike passage and Fargo rode slowly, scanning the ground, suddenly reined up as the marks were clear in front of him. No covering their trail, now, he grunted to himself as he read the hoofprints. Unshod horses, short-strided animals, Apache ponies, hard-muscled and tough. He saw the double row of tracks, fifteen riders, he guessed, perhaps a few more. One set of tracks cut across the

146

ground to vanish into the high rocks on the other side, the other set turned into the rocks at his left.

He could piece together the picture. They'd had a scout out and he had watched the herd, then fetched the main party after a few days. They had come in here and taken up their positions someplace. He took the Sharps from its saddle holster, held it in the crook of his arm, and slowly circled back, not glancing up at the rocks on either side. He'd returned back less than half a mile when he saw the herd moving toward him, Norbert in front, Henrietta Baker beside him. Fargo hauled up before them.

"We've got company," he said softly.

"Apache?" Henrietta asked.

"In the high rocks." He nodded.

"They watching us now?" Ed Norbert asked.

"You can be sure of it," Fargo answered. "Looking and counting."

"The steers?" the man asked.

"Hell, no. The Apache don't give a damn about the steers. The women and the horses, that's what they're counting," Fargo said.

"We just sit and wait for them to come down on us?" Norbert said.

"No, you make like you don't even know they're there. You remember all that old stock I told you to bring along?" Fargo asked and the man nodded.

"Take the others and cut them out of the herd. When you've cut them out, move them to the front of the herd. Don't hurry, just cut them out normal-like, change them around in the herd, and bring them up front. The Apache will wait and watch. They'll be curious enough for that."

Norbert nodded again and Henrietta Baker rode off with him as he gathered the others to help. Fargo moved slowly in front, watching, and when they had finished he guessed they had about twenty of the old, extra stock. "Move on, slow and easy. Keep the wagons close together, bring them up at the rear," he instructed. He took his place in the lead, Ed Norbert and Henrietta Baker behind him, the Sturdivents behind them. The Downer boys, Cassie and Carrie, rode herd on the flanks of the steers, Sandra and Bobby just before the wagons. He saw Amanda Koster on her horse alongside the wagon with Sophie driving.

They had gone perhaps another half-mile when Fargo caught the movement on the top line of the rocks as the line of figures appeared, each one on his pony. He counted seven on one side of the rocks, eight on the other. Fargo raised his hand and the herd came to a rumbling halt. The figures atop the rocks sat absolutely motionless. They might have been a part of the rocks to a casual observer. Fargo picked out the leader, carrying a lance and wearing a wrist cuff fringed with buckskin thongs and decorated with beadwork. His eyes went over the others, all holding their short, powerful bows in one hand.

Fargo's glance went back to his people, saw the tightness in each face. Liz sat her bay just back of Barney on the chuck wagon, watching the figures on the rocks along with everyone else. Sandra sat her horse with a rifle across her lap, as did the others, but Fargo felt the grimness grow inside him as he surveyed the group. With the attack on Haskell's men they'd had time to set themselves, pick a target, and take careful aim. It was almost like shooting sitting ducks. An Apache attack would be very different. Survival was suddenly beginning to seem damn slim.

"We just going to wait here?" he heard Norbert say, the man's voice strained.

Fargo nodded. "Shooting on the run won't help us any," he said. He sat quietly on the pinto and the minutes began to seem like hours. Little beads of perspiration had started to coat Ed Norbert's face, he noted, and Henrietta Baker's crackling eyes were taking on uneasiness.

"What the hell are they waiting for?" Harry Sturdivent half-whispered, his voice almost cracking.

"They're letting the pressure build up so you're all ready to fall apart when they attack. The Apache are the smartest and the cruelest warriors of all. They're the best at this kind of thing. They won't waste a man if they can get what they want without it," Fargo said.

He had just finished when he saw the one with the fringed wrist cuff raised his lance. The others turned at once, started to move down from both sides of the high rocks. But no swooping, wild attack. They filed down slowly on each side, reached the level ground to come together and form a semicircle around the forward part of the herd. The one with the lance let his horse move a few feet forward. Tall, with the dark-red cast to his skin of the Apache tribes, his black eyes glittered out of an arrogantly cruel face. He let his pony take another few steps forward, waited. Fargo responded to the unspoken gesture and moved the pinto forward. The Indian waved his lance at the others behind Fargo, brought the tip of the spear back to point at the Trailsman. Fargo understood the question and he nodded that he was spokesman for everyone.

The Apache spoke, a deep, throaty voice, and Fargo felt surprise as he heard the words in English. "Women. Horses," the man said. He gestured to Fargo's magnificent Ovaro. "That one," he said. His eyes went to Norbert's and he nodded, passed over the steed Henrietta sat. "That one," he said, indicating Harry Sturdivent's horse. He fastened his eyes on Liz's bay and Bobby Dodd's horse, gestured to both.

Fargo said nothing as the Apache brought his eyes back to him. The Indian raised his lance, pointed to

Cassie and Carrie, his eyes moving back to Fargo. "All rest go on," the Indian said.

Fargo gave no answering sign and the Apache backed his pony until he had taken his place in line again with the others. "What's he doing, now?" Norbert asked.

"Giving us time to think," Fargo said. "Five horses, Cassie and Carrie against everybody else's life. He's offered us a bargain in his eyes."

Fargo's glance moved slowly across the others and he saw the dilemma whirling behind each face as they stared back at him. "My God, you can't say yes, Fargo," the Reverend called out.

"I'm not calling this one," Fargo said, his eyes going to Norbert.

"I don't know," the man admitted honestly. "I'll say it for everybody else. I want to tell them to go to hell but what are our chances?"

"Damn slim," Fargo said honestly.

"I don't know," the man repeated. "It's easy to say no to them but we've come a long way to commit suicide. I don't know and I hate myself for being that way but there's no time left for anything but being honest." Norbert stared at the Trailsman and Fargo gave him credit for being open about the thoughts he knew whirled inside the others.

"No, you can't," he heard the Reverend boom out.

"I say no, tell them to go to hell," Henrietta Baker snapped. "But I'm an old woman. I've not a lot left to lose but a few years."

"I want to know what Fargo says," Barney McCall called out. Fargo's eyes went to Cassie and Carrie. Their eyes watched him round with uncertainty and apprehension, their frowns staying on him with a kind of shocked disbelief.

"I'm not giving them my pinto," Fargo said, let a slow grin slide across his face as his eyes stayed on the twins. He watched long breaths slide from them and Carrie's lips start to form a tiny smile.

"You're rotten, Fargo," she whispered, a tiny giggle following.

"Wonderful rotten," the other echoed.

"That's good enough for me," Norbert said.

"Let's see if I can deal some," Fargo said, moved the pinto forward. The Apache came out to meet him at once. "No women. Three horses," Fargo said.

He saw the Apache's face harden, his black eyes grow smaller. "One woman, three horses," he said. "No more talk." Fargo watched the Indian spin the pony around and return to the others. He started to move back to Norbert and Henrietta with a half-shrug. They had all heard the Indian's final answer and he'd no need to say more. The movement at the side of the herd caught his eye and he shot a glance in the direction, glimpsed Liz on the bay streaking around the flank of the herd. She spurred the horse forward and he whirled as she raced out toward the line of Apache. He saw the Indians react, raise their bows, but the leader held his lance sideways. Liz reined up before him, swung from the saddle, patted the bay, and stood before the Apache.

"Goddamn little fool," Fargo heard himself mutter.

The Apache took the horse's reins, motioned to one of the other Indians. The brave reached down, caught Liz by the arm, and pulled her onto his pony. "Goddamn," Fargo muttered again as the Apache flung a last glance back at them, started to lead the others back into the rocks. The brace with Liz disappeared from view and Fargo heard Harry Sturdivent's voice cry out.

"Now, what'd she go and do that for?" the man said.

"You need to ask?" Fargo said angrily. "Making up for herself. Making up to all of you."

151

"We didn't ask a damn-fool thing like that," the man protested.

"The asking was her own, the pain eating away inside her," Fargo said.

"Now what?" Amanda Koster called out. "Is there anything we can do?"

"Not you. Maybe I've a chance," Fargo said. "Maybe." His lips drew back tightly as he let thoughts race. "I'm sure as hell going to give it a try. They won't be satisfied with her, anyway. They'll have their fun with her and then come after us again."

"What can we do?" Norbert asked.

"They won't expect anyone moving right after them," he said. "If I can hit and run with her I'll be coming back hell-bent-for-leather and they'll be on my tail," he told the others. "When you see me, you stampede the herd. Blast off a volley in their ears and that'll do it. You've the old, extra stock in the front now. Stampede them straight at the Apache. Line up behind the wagons, race after the herd, and shoot your damn heads off."

He didn't wait for answers, spurred the pinto on, and raced up into the rocks. He moved in a circle, taking a passageway to bring him up high behind the route the Indians had gone. They wouldn't be hurrying, he knew, and they'd not go too far off. He moved along small, creviced pathways on the high rocks, picked up their trail with ease, followed as they moved along a narrow passageway, then up to a high place and down the other side. He halted behind a tall rock as he caught the sound of voices. Carefully, he eased the pinto foward until he could see down into a rock-lined clearing.

They had halted to examine their gift, the Apache leader standing in front of Liz, the others gathered around. They were a good twenty seconds from their ponies, he saw with grim satisfaction. He watched the

152

Apache leader take his hands and tear off Liz's blouse. The saucy, upturned little breasts came free at once and he saw the girl continue to stand with head held high. The Apache let his hand squeeze her breasts and he laughed, said something Fargo couldn't catch to the others. They joined in his laughter. Fargo drew the Colt, took careful aim, lowered the gun. The shot would bring down the Apache but it'd send the others racing for their ponies. It would cut down surprise by at least twenty seconds.

He kept the Colt in his hand as he backed the pinto a half-dozen feet, kicked hard at the horse's ribcage. The pinto responded with instant anger at the un-usued to treatment, shot forward in full gallop. Fargo saw the astonishment on their faces as he hurtled into the little clearing, leaned over, scooped Liz up with one hand. She swung herself in the saddle behind him, arms fastened around his waist as he raced into the passageway opposite. He heard the Apache shouts as they raced for their ponies. He half-turned in the saddle as he reached the passageway, fired one shot back, saw one of the braves as he just swung onto his pony, arms flying up, his body arching backward to topple from the horse.

"One less," Fargo muttered as he raced through the passageway, veered down another, found a third that led all the way down to the flat land. The sound of their ponies racing after him echoed amid the rocks and as he reached the bottom he bent low in the saddle. "Flatten down," he yelled at Liz, felt her head press against his back as she stretched her legs out across the pinto's rump.

In the distance, he saw the herd and then the fusil-lade of shots rang out. He could see the steers in-stantly begin to run, gathering speed. A half-dozen arrows whistled over his head and he managed a glance backward. The Apache had moved fast, were barrelling along behind him. He held the pinto racing straight and now the steers were a thundering stampede, a mass of dark forms hurtling at him. He waited another moment, then pulled the pinto hard, the horse whirling to the right. He reached the right edge of the stampeding herd just as they thundered past him, turned again, and galloped along the edge of the mass of racing steers.

He saw the Apache rein up, send a flurry of arrows into the first of the herd, then another in a desperate effort to halt the charging animals. It was partly as successful as he thought it would be, as a line of steers went down and others behind fell over them. The main body of the herd pressed on, climbing over the fallen bodies of the old steers, separating, but still driving on. However, it had gone as he'd hoped, halting the Apache, keeping them busy for precious seconds.

He whirled the pinto around, dumped Liz from the saddle, and yanked the Sharps out as he heard Norbert and the other firing. He saw three of the Apache go down but now the others raced to the sides to avoid the thundering herd and the gunfire that followed. He took aim, brought down an Indian that raced along the side nearest him, saw the man fall into the thundering steers. Across the way, the Apache chief had managed to regroup some of his warriors and they galloped single file, low in the saddle, firing arrows into the wagons, and the riders clustered around them. Fargo raced along the other side paralleling the Apache, saw one go down, came around behind the wagons as the Apache leader rounded on his side.

He saw the man race at him, lance upraised. Fargo halted the pinto, took aim. The lance shot through the air and he ducked, held fire as it passed less than an inch over his head. The Indian, buck knife in hand, was rising in the saddle, almost on him, preparing to leap. Fargo swung the stock of the heavy Sharps. It caught the Apache on the jaw as the Indian leaped and Fargo saw his form hit the side of the pinto, go down to the ground, the knife still in his hand. The Apache tried to raise his hand to bring the blade in for a thrust into the Ovaro's magnificent hide. Fargo fired and saw the man's face disappear in a shower of bone and blood.

He wheeled the pinto, started forward, saw three of the Apache racing away, two more on the ground. The Downer boys were reining up, waved at him. "Take the Sturdivents and Bobby, go after the herd," Fargo called. "They'll be running down soon. Keep them together. We'll catch up to you."

The boys rode off at once and Fargo saw Liz walking toward the wagons, slowly coming in from the other side, her face grave. He moved to her. "You're a damn fool," he said angrily.

"I had to do something. I tried." She shrugged helplessly. "You shouldn't have come after me."

"I hate waste," he bit out and she frowned at him. "You weren't enough. They'd have come at us again."

She stood with hands folded and Fargo saw Mrs. Downer climb from her wagon, Sandra beside her. They walked to Liz and the older woman put her arms around the girl. Sandra beside her, they took her between them, back to where the others were beginning to gather. Fargo rode up, his face still grim. "They didn't miss with every one of those damn arrows," he said.

Barney McCall nodded, turned, and Fargo followed his glance. Amanda Koster lay beside the wagon, her big head against the wheel, three arrows through her. Sophie sprawled on the driver's seat, two arrows in her, one pinning a blond braid to her breast. "Damn," Fargo murmured. "Anybody else?"

"Henrietta's got a leg wound but she's all right. Harry Sturdivent won't be using his left arm for a while," the man said.

Fargo looked at Amanda Koster and the girl. "One grave," he said. "They'll like that." He turned away, found Ed Norbert banding Sturdivent's hand. "Move on when you're finished," he said. "We've a herd to get to market."

He turned away to see Liz coming toward him, her green eyes dark with a kind of relief mixed with the pain that would take time to erase. "I keep on owing you," she said. "Only now I want to pay up."

"Maybe when it's all over," he said.

"No maybe," she said.

"All right, no maybe," he agreed with a smile. She walked off and he pointed the pinto south toward the Rio Grande.

=== 9 ===

They reached Socorra four days later, crossed the Rio Grande at a low-tide hour and a sandbar. The old, extra stock had been used up in the Apache attack and Barney McCall came to give him the rest of the money when they'd finished selling the herd. "How'd you figure you'd use the extra stock that way?" the man asked.

"I didn't but I figured they'd come in handy in some way," Fargo told him and the man went off shaking his head. He saw Liz come toward him, waited.

"It's over," she said, letting the rest of it hang.

"Go home," he said. "I haven't forgotten."

He saw her eyes widen happily. "You riding back with us?" she asked.

"No," he told her. "You'll cut over into the top of the Texas Territory and go back up the Abilene Trail. It'll be safer. I told Norbert the way."

She frowned at him. "But you just said . . ." she began.

He cut her off. "I said go home," he snapped.

Her lips tightened. "Dammit, Fargo, you still can't give an answer," she said.

"And you still ask too many questions," he told her. "Now get moving."

She stalked away, her quick temper drawn around her. The others came to say good-bye to him, each in his own way. "Ed Norbert's asked if he might come to see me when we get back," Sandra told him and he smiled for her.

"Come visit us?" Cassie and Carrie asked.

"Maybe," Fargo said and they went off giggling.

"You're a good man," Henrietta Baker told him. "Now that you've learned about antiques."

"Yes, ma'am." He laughed. He swung onto the pinto finally, headed the horse north. He rode at a steady pace, moving at an angle across New Mexico. Riding alone, he set his own pace, made steady, ground-eating time. Finally, he emerged to cut across the bottom corner of the Colorado Territory and into Kansas. He continued on, resting only when the body insisted. It was night when he moved into the center of Kansas and crossed the Smoky Hill River.

He dismounted as the dark outlines of Blakelock Haskell's place came into view. Going forward on foot, he saw the small, dim lamplight on in the living-room window. He came nearer from the side, paused to scan the area by the bushes near the front of the house. Waiting on one knee, he continued to watch the dark bushes and he smiled as he saw the tiny flare of a cigarette being lighted. He moved in a crouch, to the corner of the house, stayed low and on feet as silent as that of bobcat on the prowl, moved toward the tiny flickering pinpoint of light. The figure took shape behind it, a man with a rifle resting in the bushes. Fargo reached him before the man heard a sound. The cigarette fell from the man's lips as Fargo's arm tightened around his neck, a quick, sharp pressure. The man went limp, slid to the ground as Fargo caught the rifle.

He took it with him as he went to the front door, pushed gently on it, felt it swing open. He stepped into the dim hallway, the little lamp sending out tiny fingers of light from the living room. He saw the gray-white mane of Blakelock Haskell behind the desk, a big Walker Colt lying on the blotter in front of him. Fargo's figure stepped into the doorway and Blakelock Haskell looked up, astonishment flooding his face. His hand started for the revolver.

"Don't try it," Fargo said quietly.

The man sat back in the chair, his eyes holding hate and resignation in them. "Damn you, Fargo," he murmured. "Damn your stinking hide."

"I didn't have a hold on it for some while," Fargo said. "Not even after you had those two whores try to stampede the herd. We were moving to Colorado then but I figured you might have had somebody watching us."

"When did you put it together?" the man asked.

"After you rounded the herd up again. You were heading them down into New Mexico. You'd have taken them back toward Abilene but you'd heard we had a market waiting in New Mexico," Fargo said. "Blanche," he grunted. "I'd told her that."

"I could've heard about the New Mexico market on my own," the man protested.

"You could have, but then all the other little things began to come together," Fargo said. "You were holding off hiring hands for over a week. When Blanche made that five-thousand deposit in her special fund you did your hiring that day." The man said nothing, his eyes baleful. "All the money for your operation came from Blanche," Fargo said. "She stayed nicely to herself and fed you the money to do your thing. That way she stayed clean and had control of whatever you made."

"I'm going to kill you, Fargo," Blakelock Haskell said.

"Blanche at her place?" Fargo asked.

"She's right here, Fargo," the voice said and the half-turned, saw the woman step from the shadows of a doorway, the revolver in her hand. "Put the rifle down on the desk, Fargo," she said.

Fargo allowed a wry smile as he put the rifle across a corner of the desk. "My mistake," he said softly. "I didn't expect you'd be here."

The gray-mist eyes were exactly as he remembered them, warm and cool at once. "I've been waiting here every night since Blakelock got back and told me all that had happened," she said. "I told him not to depend on that stupid guard outside. He just never listens." She smiled. "I put my faith in you, Fargo," she said.

"Thanks," he commented.

"You should have listened to me," she said almost sadly.

"I should have listened to Liz Ryan," Fargo said and her brows lifted a fraction. "Skunks are skunks, she said, no matter what part of the family tree they come from."

The woman smiled. "Quaint," she said coldly.

"I get to kill him," Blakelock Haskell said, his voice rising. Fargo's eyes measured the distance to Blanche and the gun held steadily in her hand. Too far, he murmured silently. He saw Blakelock get to his feet, reach out, and pick up the big Walker Colt. The man moved around the corner of the desk. For a moment, he crossed in front of Blanche, blocking her. Fargo dived, yanking the rifle from the desk top with him, landed behind the desk. He fired one shot, shattered the lamp to plunge the room into darkness.

"Goddamn," he heard Haskell roar and fire off two shots. They slammed into the desk and the wall as Fargo scooted back. "I'll kill you," the man shouted again, fired off another two shots in the darkness. Fargo followed the flash of the gun, pulled the trigger of the rifle, and Blakelock Haskell's voice screamed in pain. The scream became a gutteral rasp of agony and Fargo heard the man fall against the desk, his breath wheezing, then the heavy sound of his body crashing to the floor. A flitting shape flashed through the doorway and Fargo leaped to his feet. He ran, halted, peered around the doorway, and heard her footsteps outside, running. He followed at once.

She was at the horse, one foot in the stirrup as he ran to stand in the open doorway. "Hold it there," he said quietly. Blanche slowly brought her leg down, began to turn toward him. His eyes watched, peered, expecting, and then he saw it, the dull sheen for an instant as the pistol, still in her hand, came around. He leaped to one side as she fired, the bullet ploughing into the door frame. His finger pressed the rifle trigger, an instant, automatic reaction, and the rifle exploded.

Blanche Haskell gave a short, gasping scream. She began to bow forward, almost as if she were curtsying, took a single step, and collapsed to the ground, the gun falling from her hand. The front of her dress was already soaked in red as he reached her and the mist-gray eyes stared up at him.

"Blakelock was always so stupid," she murmured.

"He wasn't the only one," Fargo said grimly.

A small sound left her. He thought it sounded like a wry laugh as the mist-gray eyes closed.

Fargo rose, threw the rifle into the bushes. Greed, he murmured to himself. It demanded a full price. He walked slowly to the pinto and rode to Rawley. He took the same room in the single hotel, slept for three days, except for time to eat and consume a bottle of bourbon. Finally he rose, washed, rode off, made his way to the small spread over the hills. She'd have had time to return and he realized he was peering anxiously as he came in sight of the house.

The lithe, slender form appeared in the doorway as he swung down from the pinto, her high-planed handsomeness almost beautiful. "It's done with once and for all," he said.

"I know," she said. "We got back yesterday. It's all over town. They think it was a family falling-out. I knew better the minute I heard."

"Where's Barney?" he asked her.

"Gone to buy new stock, be back next week," she said, closing the door behind him as he stepped into the cabin. She began to unbutton her shirt and the sharp, saucy breasts came into view. Size and beauty weren't the same at all, he realized once again. There was always time to ride on. It promised to be a damn fine week.

LOOKING FORWARD!

The following is the opening section
from the next novel in the exciting
Trailsman series from Signet:

THE TRAILSMAN #9: DEAD MAN'S SADDLE

*The town of Condor,
where the Texas Territory
and Mexico nudged each other,
in the early 1860's.*

Fargo opened the door to the hotel room and halted in surprise. They'd told him he had a visitor waiting but he'd expected the Army sergeant making another pitch. He let his eyebrows lift as he took in the girl, deep strawberry-blond hair pulled back a little severely, tall, long legs enclosed in riding breeches, a buckskin vest over a tan blouse that couldn't completely hold down the soft curve of full breasts. He scanned her face, deeply tanned, a nice nose, full lips, soft blue eyes, a pretty face able to look very firm and businesslike, as it did now.

"Sorry to surprise you like this," she said, her voice soft, and she allowed a little smile to soften her face. "I've come to try to persuade you," she said.

"The Army send you?" He frowned incredulously.

"No, I'm here on my own account. I'm Fern Blake," she said.

His eyes took in her figure again, returned to her face. Very nice, he decided. "How do you figure to persuade me?" he asked. "With clothes on or clothes off?"

He saw her lips draw in for a moment. "With clothes on," she said coolly.

"That's going to make it a lot harder." He smiled amiably.

"A thousand dollars," she said. "That ought to take care of persuading."

Fargo let his eyes study her.

"What do you say?" she asked.

"I say I'm getting curious as all hell," he answered. "First this apple-cheeked young sergeant comes up and tells me the Army wants me to do a job for them, double the usual civilian scout's pay. I tell him I'm not interested and he says it's my patriotic duty and he's authorized to make it triple the usual pay. Now you're here offering a hell of a lot more, only you're not the Army, you're here on your own."

"It must be somewhat unsettling." She smiled. She was trying to be coolly pleasant, he saw, but something bubbled deep inside her. He caught the way her fingers moved nervously on the edge of the small leather purse she had over one shoulder.

"I don't unsettle easy but why don't you tell me what the hell this is all about, honey," he said.

"Fern Blake," she corrected.

"All right, Fern. That's a nice name. Now talk," he said.

She looked uncomfortable for a moment. "You were told it was a scouting assignment. That's all I can say until you agree to take the job," she said.

"Then you can go persuade somebody else, Fern, honey," he said affably.

"There is no one like you. You are the best, I'm told," she said. He shrugged, made no comment. "I've offered a lot of money," she said.

"You have," he agreed. "But then money never did persuade me much about anything."

She shot him a distinctly annoyed frown. "Are you saying that if I persuaded you with my clothes off you'd agree?" she asked.

"No, but I'd enjoy it more," he said. "Try me." He smiled. "You never know."

"I have the impression you're more interested in that than the job," she said disapprovingly.

"You get the cigar, honey." He smiled.

"Fern," she snapped.

"Fern," he said agreeably.

He saw her shrug in dismay, her hand move under the buckskin vest. It came out holding a small pistol, a rim-fire European model but deadly enough at this close range. "I'm afraid I'll have to use this kind of persuasion, then," she said.

He eyed the gun again. "You're full of surprises, aren't you?" he said.

"Take your gun from the holster," she ordered. "Use two fingers only." She backed a few paces, kept the little pistol leveled at him. "The gun, please," Fern Blake said sharply.

"You won't use that popgun, honey," Fargo said calmly.

"I certainly will," she retorted indignantly.

He shook his head. "I can't do you much good dead, now can I?" he said affably, saw her mouth fall open for a second. It was a reply she hadn't thought about. She blinked, the gun still on him, and he heard the sound of footsteps approaching in the hallway, two pairs of boots. His hand went to the holster. "They come in this room they're dead men," he said.

He saw Fern Blake hesitate, and then her voice called out sharply. "No, stay there. Don't come in," she said.

"You in trouble?" Fargo heard the voice call out.

"No," the girl said. "I'm all right. Stay outside." Fargo heard the quiver in her voice, uncertainty and dismay in it. The men outside caught it also. His eyes were on the door as it crashed open, the two men rushing in after it, guns in hand. Fargo had the big Colt in his hand before the door had half-opened. He fired twice, the two shots so fast they seemed one. The two men hit each other as they fell backward, collapsing into the hallway with twin stains of red spreading from their chests.

Fargo turned to Fern Blake, the Colt in his hand. She was staring out at the two figures lying half atop each other in the hallway, her face white, drawn. "I told them to let me handle it," she gasped out. "I told them."

"They should have listened to you," Fargo said casually. "Now give me that popgun." She brought her eyes to him and he saw refusal there. "I can make it three," he said.

"You wouldn't," she gasped out, watched his eyes, and swallowed hard, reached her hand out to give him the gun. He flipped it on its side, emptied the two shells, and tossed it back to her. More footsteps pounded outside and others appeared in the hallway. He saw a figure push its way through, a beefy man wearing a sheriff's badge.

"They tried to rob the lady and me," Fargo said, glanced at Fern Blake.

She blinked, shook her head. "Yes, yes, that's right," she said.

The sheriff looked down at the two men. "Anybody know them?" he asked. No one answered. "Never saw them before, either," the man grumbled. "All right, get 'em out of here."

Fargo grunted as he shut the door. Condor was a

town that was like this land, a place where life and death were only passing moments. There was law, but not much of it. Mostly there was the fight to find a place to survive in a land that was still torn between two countries, a place of divided loyalties and no loyalties at all. He'd led a party of land speculators down here and he had no desire to stay. He turned to Fern Blake.

"Now you can start persuading me with your clothes off," he said.

Her eyes grew wide, fear leaping in their soft blue centers. "No, you wouldn't," she said.

"Either that or you start telling me what the hell this is all about," he barked.

She drew a deep breath and the tan vest moved an inch out further. "All right," she almost whispered. "But not here, not now. Tonight. I want somebody else there to meet you," she said. "I'm staying at a little place just south of Condor. Ride along Mesa road and you can't miss it."

"If you're trying to set me up again you're going to be the prettiest corpse this side of the border," Fargo said harshly. Her eyes were wide but he saw no duplicity in them. Her hand reached out, touched his for a moment, drew back at once.

"No tricks, I promise," she said. "I'm sorry about this, all of it. It just went all wrong, even my part. It was a bad idea, all of it," she said.

"I'd agree with that," he said.

"Nine o'clock," she said and he nodded. She moved to the door, paused, looked back at him. She was really damn good-looking, he decided, and wondered what in the hell she was into. "I'm sorry, really I am," she offered.

"We'll see," was all he allowed her. He watched her